A Brief History of Several Boyfriends

Stories

Janet Olearski

*For my parents, who advised me about boyfriends
as best they could.*

Table of Contents

'First ambitions are best. We are less brave later. Don't you think?'
'Or we simply change?'

Andrew Miller, Pure

Just What the Doctor Ordered

WHAT HE TOLD her was that he and his wife lived apart. She in Paris, he in the Gulf. He had a successful practice and it afforded him a pleasant and relaxing lifestyle, whilst providing ample funding for his daughter's education.

His wife had precious little time for him. She flew in with their daughter for Christmas and Easter and flew back out again at the earliest opportunity. She was tolerant and worldly, and she welcomed his girlfriends with graciousness. He, on the other hand, bestowed only a version of meanness on his girlfriends, all of whom he held in thrall with some inexplicable power. Tess was no exception.

In Tess, Gilbert – for that was his name – had realised he was on to a good thing, and that good thing was Tess. In her obsession, infatuation, love blindness – call it what you will – she gave of herself so as not to appear ungenerous, but especially to please. In giving, she was buying Gilbert's affections. He in turn would rarely put his hand into his pocket – metaphorically or otherwise – for anyone.

Gilbert's regard for Tess was paralleled only by his disdain for his patients. His belief was that they were the cause of their own ailments. He railed at them for their bloated bodies, their untutored eating habits, their minor excesses. They trembled at his judgements, but they did not baulk at paying his inflated bills.

During his wife's absences, Tess would fetch and carry for him. He would send her to the supermarket with a long list of items for purchase. She would hurry there in her car, filled with a sense of purpose. She had been sent on an important mission and was determined to excel. She would bustle about buying things she normally never bought, cuts of meat, charcuterie, unique imported sauces, creams for whipping and pouring, smoked salmon, streaky bacon not too fat, spices, but not fruits, since Gilbert abhorred fruits. What Gilbert could do well was cook. Tess, who could not cook, was his bottle-washer.

When Tess was halfway through her shopping list, Gilbert – as if prompted by second sight – would call her … and ask for more. Could she bring him this brand or that? Could she bring him some chicken livers, or a side of pork, or some shallots or artichokes, some black olives – the provenance of which was always important. And then, when Tess reached the cash desk, she would pay with her credit card – huge amounts because she would also throw in little extras, special treats for the person who never treated her.

And that evening, as a bonus, Tess would buy him dinner. Not an insignificant dinner in a local cafe, but rather a dinner of many courses with aperitifs and a couple of bottles of imported wine. The digestivos were usually offered on the house to these clients who had consumed so much. The restaurant staff welcomed them like long-lost friends; people came to their table to greet them. There was a great deal of shaking of hands and chatting. Gilbert would comment about people he had spotted. This one with the wife who had a large bottom – *masha'allah*! The husband was having an affair with the skinny woman to his right, but his wife had her secrets too. He would spot a government minister who was with a woman who was not his wife. He would hiss and mumble about him. Then, when the minister passed by, Gilbert would stand up and shake his hand vigorously and engage in an exchange of anecdotes. At the end of the evening, when the bill came, Tess paid. She always picked up the bill. Gilbert would never have taken her out and paid, or if he had done, he would have taken her somewhere cheaper.

In later years, looking back at that time, Tess thought that perhaps she could have bought herself a new car or paid mortgage instalments on a house, or at least invested the money spent on Gilbert in an offshore account. She considered also that sometimes people do bad things to you and that you don't notice until years later. Why was it, she wondered, that while he was being so mean to her, she simply didn't see it? One of the mysteries of life.

Gilbert was not special in any special way. Tess was the first to acknowledge this. He had something, a certain charisma – clearly a lot to have attracted the likes of her. But he would be moody too. He resented her interventions in the kitchen. She was useless and stupid, or so he said. Her aspirations were *also* stupid and over time she ceased to discuss them. He was right on one score. With regard to him, she was very, very stupid indeed, foolish not to have offloaded him at her earliest convenience.

Something happened.

She had bought gifts at Christmas for him, for his wife, and for his daughter. By buying gifts for Gilbert's wife and daughter, Tess was again trying to curry favour with Gilbert himself. As always, she observed the protocol – to call, to announce that she was in town and to ask if she might 'pop round.' It was a little like asking permission to enter her own home. She had some gifts for them, she said.

Gilbert instructed her that he would call her back. But he didn't. The weekend passed. There was no call and Tess waited alone in her hotel, reading distractedly by the pool, watching old soaps and movies on TV, and all the time checking her phone for missed calls. In the end, she returned home, carrying with her the chocolates and the champagne, the gifts they might well have enjoyed together, the four of them. At home, she placed the packages on her sideboard, viewing them each day as she entered and exited her apartment.

After several days had passed, and she sat on her sofa watching as the coloured flicker of the fireworks outside were reflected in her TV screen, she saw herself as she actually was … a woman sitting alone on a sofa in her apartment in front of a TV screen. It occurred to her at that moment, in a state of extreme lucidity, that the one thing she would not need in life was a doctor.

What, then, of the undelivered gifts?

Postcard

In some distant country, in the back of beyond, when Christina stood pushing her postcards into an empty metal post box, hearing them clatter onto its hollow floor, she remembered Sonia. Sonia flitted into her mind like a soul without a home.

It was Sonia who had appeared in shows, auditioned, sung at concerts, and travelled to film studios together with Christina's grandmother Kay. The two women, Sonia and Kay, had been almost inseparable. Sonia was not at all flamboyant in the way that Kay had been, but she was of the same essence. Theatricality is in the blood, they say. Except everyone ruled that out when they met Christina.

Christina thought back to the winter when Sonia had contacted her mother. It had been agreed that she and her mother should pay a visit. Christina was not especially keen. She worried that her mother might be showing her off, and that Sonia would be expecting her to be just like her grandmother. It seemed to Christina that she would disappoint them both. She protested, but her mother had got it into her head that they had to go and was ready for a stroll down memory lane. Christina sulked – as she did in those days – but they went anyway.

Over time, people lose the details of experiences and events. They think they'll remember, but they don't. Those details are gone. When she looked back, Christina could not recall if the day of that meeting they had taken the bus one stop too far, or not far enough. She had studied the relevant pages from the *A to Z*, turning it sideways and upside down to get her bearings. Her mother tried to spot street names as the bus trundled along under an overcast sky. When they finally arrived, they found Sonia there in the street waiting for them, concerned they might get lost. She had come out into the cold to find them and guide them back to her front room, where tea in fine rose-patterned china cups and Viennese cakes on matching plates awaited.

It was at a time when Christina must have been at university, or perhaps was about to go. She was journeying back and forth to stay in some arid Calabrian coastal town, to be with a man, pointlessly so. It was all costing a good bit of money. The man was having fine times at Christina's expense.

'I wish I could have done the same at her age,' her mother would say, learning that Christina was off again to Italy – as if this were an acceptable thing, a young woman taking herself away to visit a man who never once thought to come and visit her. That was part of Christina's embarrassment. She had nothing to report to Sonia, only that she had a boyfriend from there. She had enough sense not to let slip that Kay's granddaughter was seeing a man who was separated, but not yet divorced. And him a foreigner at that. Years later it pained her to think about it. Sometimes people know things are wrong and, because they're wrong, the 'being wrong' isolates them. They're slapped over with the paint of guilt and it won't wash off.

When they got into the light and warmth of the flat, Sonia couldn't take her eyes off Christina. She was looking for the resemblance, almost in awe. Christina could not gauge how much she did, or did not, look like her grandmother. That was for others to perceive. Christina reminded Sonia of someone. It was partly Kay, but it was also someone else. Sonia stared and thought as she poured the tea. In an armchair, in a corner of the room, sat her husband, reading his newspaper.

'Who does Christina remind you of, Bernard?' she asked him more than once. Bernard looked at Christina over his glasses, said nothing, and continued reading.

Christina was drawn into an interrogation for which she was ill-prepared. Sonia wanted to hear all about how much she liked Calabria. In truth Christina hated it, but could not say. She only went because of the man. Sonia wanted hear about Christina's interests, her studies, her aspirations. Everything had seemed perfectly clear until Sonia had asked her. How could she answer when she did not really know? She didn't know her own mind either, which was worse. When she thought back to that time, she did not despise the Christina of the past for her ignorance. She felt compassion for her.

In the midst of this, there was a sudden flash of recognition in Sonia's expression. She knew without a shadow of a doubt who it was Christina reminded her of.

'Vivien Leigh!' she said. 'That's who you look like. A young Vivien Leigh.'

Christina was immediately evaluated by three pairs of eyes.

'Who?' said Christina.

'Can't you see it, Bernard?' Sonia said, turning to her husband. 'Vivien Leigh, *Gone With The Wind*. Remember?'

He rattled his newspaper. 'Maybe,' he conceded.

'Look,' said Sonia to Christina's mother, 'can't you see it? The similarity.'

Christina's mother was flattered, if not surprised, that a daughter of hers should have come out looking like Vivien Leigh.

'Oh yes!' she said, seeing it for the first time.

'Oh yes,' said Sonia. 'Definitely Vivien Leigh!'

And there were the two of them staring at Christina, admiring her, wondering at the coincidence.

'It's the eyes,' said Sonia, 'and the shape of her face ...' Christina could have been Vivien Leigh's stand-in. Sonia knew. She had worked on *Ship of Fools* and had seen the real Vivien. So, who could argue with her? But there was something demeaning about being compared to someone who, even at Christina's age, was renowned, when Christina herself was not, and probably never would be. Christina was the first insignificant one of her kind, but the millionth Vivien Leigh look-alike. There's something not quite right about that. But not to Sonia's mind. It brought her immense pleasure this discovery.

So, a scene in Sonia's front room: Christina and her mother sipping their Earl Grey and eating dainty European pastries; Bernard sitting in his armchair and reading his newspaper, glancing from time to time at the visitors without saying a word; Sonia telling them about her holidays in Capri, and how she'd sing medleys of old favourites at the piano in some Italian *trattoria* to the delight of the proprietor. And Sonia remembering Kay, her eyes becoming glassy as she considered the loss of her old friend so long gone. For a few moments, they all sat silently in that memory.

Christina knew her mother wanted to get back to give her father his dinner. Sonia urged them to stay, but they could not. Christina's mother said they would definitely come again. She would come on her own, or with Christina ... if Christina was back from Italy. She was leaving again in a few days' time. Another reason why Christina hadn't wanted to visit that day: there were things to do, a suitcase to pack. But people can always find time for the things that matter. As Christina later discovered.

Sonia hurried into another room and brought back an address book and a postcard. She had an old friend in Taormina. Perhaps when Christina got there, to wherever she was going, she would post a card to him from Sonia. Christina was not going anywhere remotely near. The card would have arrived sooner from England. Despite that, Christina agreed. Sonia was, in any case, already scribbling her message. Christina had the vaguest impression that Bernard raised his head for a moment to look in their direction.

Sonia wanted to give Christina the money. For a postcard? Christina said not to worry – she would take care of it.

And then they left, Sonia insisting on accompanying them up the road.

'You'll make yourself ill,' said Bernard. 'I'll go.'

'No, you'll make *yourself* ill,' said Sonia. 'You stay here and read your paper.'

And she went with them in the cold all the way to the bus stop, hugged them both, made them promise to come back. Christina was relieved to get away, as she always was, even years later, whenever she went to visit anyone. She was no sooner there than she wanted to be gone. And yet, in retrospect, she had enjoyed that day. She didn't know if she had enjoyed it for what had been said, or because she had done a good deed and had been there to give some satisfaction to an old lady.

The two women both came away with the sense of a job well done. Somehow, though, Christina could not really see herself returning. They watched Sonia standing in the darkness waving to them as they sat in the bus. And then they were off, heading home through the unknown territories of Hampstead. When someone doesn't own a car – and they didn't – even places that are near seem light years away. Christina would fly for three and a half hours to see her Italian, but twenty-five minutes on the bus in a freezing English winter seemed an eternity.

She took Sonia's postcard with her to Calabria. She was miles from the nearest post office, she had no transport. She relied on him. Whatever her initial intentions back in London, she did not dare ask the man about buying stamps. He didn't consider things like that important. Christina had the wrong kind of relationship with him, she realized. If she couldn't ask him to buy her a stamp, what kind of a relationship was it? On the last day, her conscience got the better of her, and she asked him. Please, she said, please could he post this card for her? It was very important.

He scrutinised the postcard and the message. He sat for a long time trying to decipher it. Every so often he looked up at her, then back again at the card. His expression was stern, but otherwise deadpan. That's the way he was. But he was shut out, too, from her language and her world: he had shut himself out. Christina knew what he was thinking, that she might have written it herself ... to a secret boyfriend.

She said, 'I know what you're thinking.'

He said, 'What am I thinking?'

'That I've written the card to some man I know,' she said. 'Anyway, you can see it's not my writing.'

'Isn't it?' he said. He could be very awkward when he wanted to be.

'I'd hardly give it to you to post if it was to a boyfriend, would I?'

'You might,' he said, 'to make me jealous.'

Christina wanted to do one of her sarcastic laughs and say, 'You can't be serious,' but she didn't. Scorn was wasted on him. Either he didn't get it or he didn't want to get it. In the end he took the card and posted it. It was a game he was playing, but the trouble was Christina never knew where the game began and where it ended. And that was always the problem.

Back in England, Bernard phoned Christina's mother. He told her Sonia had collapsed and died just the week after their visit. He had not known where to lay his hands on their number. In the end, he had found it in one of Sonia's address books, but by the time Christina's mother had had the news, Sonia was dead and buried. And it was probably around that time that Sonia's postcard, her last postcard, had reached its destination.

⊷⊶

'Did you ever post that card for her?' Christina's mother, increasingly forgetful, often asked her daughter. And Christina, whose trips now were always for business, never for pleasure, thought how the recipient, whoever he was, had had a postcard from a dead woman, sent on her behalf by a poor imitation of a deceased film star.

But the Christina of those times was long gone, of course.

⊷⊶

Designer Baby

The interview had gone rather well, she thought. She had sent Taylor the link and, within a short arc of time, he had called her.

'I loved it,' he said. 'When will the program go out?'

'We haven't scheduled it yet, but we have an editorial meeting on Friday. That's when I'll be pulling it out of the hat. It's going to knock their socks off.'

'Really?'

'Don't be surprised. It's not every day we find someone like you.'

'How do you mean?'

'Honestly, Taylor, do you want me to spell it out for you?'

'Yes. Yes, well why not?'

She laughed.

He laughed. 'Go on,' he said.

'You're perfect,' she said. 'And dare I say it? Every woman's dream.'

'I'm blushing,' he said.

'No, you're not. Designer babies don't blush. I'm sure they don't.'

'So, you think I'm perfect. How about you come round and check me out?'

She laughed, a little uncomfortably this time. 'Well, I just want to say thank you again for doing the interview, Taylor.'

'No, seriously,' he said. 'Come over. It's an invitation. I'm cooking.'

It was a double whammy for Cassie. Not just the interview, but also a date. Admittedly, as far as the interview was concerned, she'd had some reservations. The whole idea of editing genes to produce perfect or designer babies seemed to her to be fraught with dangers. Her background research had confirmed this and she had said as much in her introduction to the piece. What were the chances of something going wrong? What about the parents who, for a massive payment, could prescribe the type of child they wanted? And what about the parents who could not? Was that fair? Was the whole business ethical anyway? And did the public know that the editing of genes had already been going on for many years … since she herself was a child? No, she assumed they didn't. She had no idea that while she was growing up as a normally conceived child, the likes of Taylor was growing up in his perfect self – with those gleaming white teeth, that miraculous physique, that remarkable brain, but also that enchanting personality of his. She was almost envious of him herself. In fact, she *was* envious. And now, added to all of that … the date.

And here she was in his penthouse apartment, chopping parsley and sipping white wine while he busied himself in his designer kitchen, preparing a romantic dinner for the two of them.

'So, editorial meeting on Friday?' said Taylor. 'You think they'll go for it?

'Absolutely.'

'Is this all your own work?'

Cassie laughed. 'It is indeed. I tracked you down,' she said, 'and I came up with the idea for the program. I wanted to gazumph them all. It's not easy in this business. It takes something really big to get their attention.' She waved her chopping knife in the air in a triumphant gesture.

Taylor moved close to her and grasped her wrist. 'Careful,' he said and she felt his warm breath on her face as he leaned in to kiss her. The knife fell from her hand. Taylor stooped to retrieve it. 'No worries,' he said, stepping back to his work. 'I guess I'm something really big then.'

'You will be when the show's released.'

'Show?'

'Program,' said Cassie. 'Show. Whatever.'

'I was just a little bit worried about what you said about the engineering not being a good idea. Do you think *I'm* not a good idea?' He continued preparing the food as he spoke.

'I think you're a very good idea,' said Cassie.

'Mmm,' he said.

Cassie slipped into place on one of Taylor's tall chrome and Perspex kitchen chairs. She crossed her legs and raised her glass to her lips. Taylor glanced at her legs then, smiling, returned his focus to the food.

'One thing I never got to find out,' said Cassie. 'Do you actually know who your father was? You sort of avoided that question in the interview.'

Taylor was silent.

Cassie gave a little cough and looked at him.

'Yes,' he said.

'Well?'

'You have to understand that mine was one of the first cases. It was experimental.' He took hold of a knife and began to chop vegetables expertly on a block. He looked up for a moment. 'Can you get a couple of small pans out of there for me?' He nodded towards the row of pristine silver-surfaced cupboards.

She followed his instructions. 'These?' she said, holding the pans up for his approval.

'You got it,' he said. 'And there's some cream in the fridge.'

She opened the voluminous fridge and looked for the cream. What she noticed were two bottles of champagne on ice. She took out the carton of cream, a great sense of satisfaction warming her heart.

'So?' she said. 'Are you going to tell me?'

'What?' His smile was so sweet, so warm.

'Your father?' She punched him playfully on the arm.

'He was a PhD.'

'Ah,' she said.

'In the Ohio State Prison.'

'No, really? What did he do there?'

Taylor had his head down as he arranged slivers of fig on a plate. 'He was an inmate. Death Row.' He looked up and smiled at her.

Cassie blinked. 'Wow,' she said, and took a sip of her wine. She swallowed. 'Wow,' she said again.

'Cassie, darling,' he said, 'could you go fetch the meat? It's in the fridge.' He leaned towards her and gave her a peck on the cheek.

Cassie walked back to the fridge and pulled open the door. She scanned the contents. Vegetables, cheeses, sauces… the champagne, of course.

'I don't see the meat,' she said. She turned. Taylor was there in front of her, still smiling.

He raised the carving knife and twirled it in front of her face. 'The meat?' he said. 'You're it.'

The Deciding Factor

I'M GOING TO tell you a story about a woman – but it could just as well have been a man – who was never quite satisfied with what she had in her life.

If she bought a dress, or if she bought some food at the supermarket, on the way home she would wonder if she should have bought something else instead: a dress of a different colour, or fish instead of meat. Sometimes she would buy two of the same thing because she didn't want to experience the anguish of doubting the wisdom of her choice.

In her teens and early twenties, she had put herself through considerable mental turmoil and caused a great deal of unhappiness to others because she couldn't decide which men she wanted to go out with. Older now, and very slightly wiser, she had concluded that by not seeing anyone, she could save herself this torment, and not be the cause of any man's misery.

Her major decisions were now fairly mundane, all – that is – except for those to do with her working life. She had a good job. Many of the people who knew her envied her for her job. She had status and even some degree of influence, though she was aware that she was underpaid for what she did. How would it be, she wondered, if she had a job of the same value, but which paid far more?

One day, while thumbing through a holiday brochure – she couldn't decide if she wanted to take a six-day holiday in February, or a fourteen-day holiday in May, and she didn't quite know if it would be better to go to a hotel in Tobago, which was relatively cheap but under-resourced, or to a hotel in Antiqua, which was expensive, but had a fitness centre, tennis courts, free scuba lessons, and evening entertainment – one day, while considering all this, she had a phone call from a man she had known now for three years or so.

Sometimes this man was there for her. Sometimes he wasn't. Initially she had been ecstatic at the idea of falling in love with just this one person but, alas, the falling-in-love just hadn't happened for the other half of this relationship, probably because he was a man who found it hard to decide if he wanted a tall woman with short hair or a short woman with long hair, or even if he wanted her blonde and business-like, or dark and home-loving. Now, after a long holiday that he had spent for the most part making similar comparisons in other sectors of his life, he was back in town and, from the comfort of his office, with his address book open on the desk in front of him, he was calling her.

She asked him about his holiday. He asked her about her job. She spoke of her current responsibilities and her potential possibilities. He told her of the red wine and the white, and how, having bought the white, he knew he should have taken the red. She told him tales of her own exploitation, and he scolded her for her readiness to be exploited. Such were their conversations. They started and they ended, and sometime later, they started and they ended again. There was continuation, and there was no continuation. For him, there was an evening to fill, which might or might not render an atmosphere of delight. He could not decide if she was for him, or if there might not perhaps be something better just around the corner: someone, possibly, that he hadn't met before, but might meet soon. For her, there was an evening to fill that might turn out like many of the others … inconclusively, with him – and yet – not with him. She wondered, as she often did of late if she should spend an evening with a man who might or might not be committed, or if she should dedicate the time to her work and further ponderings about the structure of her future.

Since neither could admit to the other that they were not able to take a decision at that moment, they agreed to contact each other the following afternoon, though it was not clear, she realized, when she had put down the receiver, whether he would call her or she should call him. However, this was a point of little significance, and it was probable, though not absolutely certain, that they would be in touch the following day.

That night the woman lay warm in her bed, between her peach-coloured sheets, rejoicing in the comfort of her solitude, but wondering what it might be like to share that haven with another. Her eyes scanned the titles of the books on the shelf opposite her bed. She often bought two or three books at a time and, since it had always been difficult for her to decide which book to read first in order to expand her knowledge and further her career, she rarely read any. Now as she contemplated which title she might consider examining that night, or perhaps the following night, her eyelids grew heavy and her thoughts talked amongst themselves of love and work and ambition and food and clothes and holidays and wine and … and … and … And she dreamt.

She dreamt a dream about a woman – but it could just as well have been a man – who was not quite satisfied with something she had bought. She found herself in a large city, at night, near closing time. Car headlights spilt through the inky darkness as she hurried along the gradually quietening streets, past the illuminated shop fronts. She was slightly breathless. Her breathlessness came from the anguish of knowing that there was little time left now before the shops closed. Even as she approached them, their shutters were pulled down and their lights switched off. Either that, or the owners and their employees were busy cashing up and wanted no more to do with last-minute customers. But, in effect, she wasn't really a customer.

Just when she had almost given up finding the right shop still open, she was there at the door. It was an off-licence. The lock was down, but she could see the assistant inside, and he could see her. She tapped on the glass and smiled.

'We're just closing,' he said, opening the door just a few inches.

'I won't be a minute,' she promised. 'I just need to change something.'

He let her in. In her hand she held a crumpled brown paper bag, and in the bag she knew there was a half-bottle of whisky.

'What do you want to change?' asked the assistant.

'I've got some whisky,' she explained, 'but it's the wrong brand. I wanted one kind, but got another by mistake.'

'What kind do you want?'

She knew exactly what she wanted, and she told him the brand name.

'What kind have you got now?' he inquired, looking down at the still unopened package.

She slipped her hand into the bag, grasped the smooth cool neck of the bottle and slid the whisky into view. The man gazed down at the label and studied it for a moment. Then, a little puzzled, he looked up.

'But,' he said, hesitating, 'the brand you want is the one you've already got.'

And so the woman awoke, and her day progressed in the way that her days progressed, except that she carried with her the vague memory of a dark street and an illuminated façade of shops, car headlights, an off-licence sign and a brown paper bag. And so it was that in the afternoon, as she pondered the images and the sounds and the feelings of that dream, she became aware of the ringing of the telephone and knew that it would be him, and that a small, rather insignificant decision was to be made. And, as she thought of that decision, she considered the many ways in which she might respond to his call.

And thinking and dreaming, she imagined a woman – but it could just as well have been a man – who was never quite satisfied with what she had in her life and who, when she heard the phone ring, was never quite sure if she should answer, because she knew there would be decisions to be made and she wasn't quite sure how she wanted them to turn out.

Crumbs

ALL HER LIFE, her father tried to control her choice of partner. He became utterly infuriating when he continued to operate that control when he was dead.

'I think,' said Mike, 'I'll decorate the kitchen. A couple of coats of paint. That should do it.'

Ruth did not look up. She liked the kitchen the way it was.

'What do you think?' he said. He was examining the walls. 'Needs a good wash first,' he said. 'What's this yellowy-brown stuff on here? Looks like cigarette smoke.'

'My dad,' said Ruth.

'Oh, I get it. He was a chain smoker,' said Mike. 'You should have put your foot down and stopped that.'

Ruth said nothing.

'Need to paint this as well,' he said, swinging the door back and forward on its hinges. A cap fell off the back of the door onto the floor. 'This isn't his cap, is it?' said Mike.

'Yes,' said Ruth.

'Not that I want to criticize,' said Mike, 'but how long has he been dead?'

'Four years,' said Ruth. 'Maybe five – yes, five.'

'Well, it's about time, don't you think?' said Mike. 'I suppose that's his coat, too.'

'Yes,' said Ruth.

'Time to move on and get rid of that stuff,' said Mike.

Ruth knew in her heart of hearts that she wasn't ready to move on. Not quite. Not yet.

That's how it started, this irritation with Mike. This take over. The planned painting of the kitchen. The advice to get rid of her dad's stuff. She wasn't having it.

It was a just a day or so later that she saw the crumbs. Mike was constantly padding about the flat, eating biscuits and miscellaneous food items rustled from the fridge and the pantry.

'Don't leave your crumbs lying around,' she told him.

'What crumbs?' he said.

Looking at the table, Ruth considered the scatter of breadcrumbs on her father's side, the side where her father sat, where her father's chair stood as it had stood all those years that he had lived in the flat.

'There,' she said and nodded towards the table.

'I never sit there,' he said. '*You* know that. It must have been you.'

She thought for a moment and then she said, 'Yes, you're right. It must have been me.' And it was her every day that followed. More breadcrumbs in the same place at the same end of the table, breadcrumbs that she swept into her hand with a silent reverence. And with the same frequency that Mike's belongings appeared randomly throughout the flat, so the crumbs appeared... as if in acknowledgement of his unwanted presence.

As she lay in bed at night, Ruth asked herself what it was that her father wanted, and did she want what her father wanted? She was, after all, her father's daughter. However much she was her own person, he was there in her blood.

Then one morning after Mike had set off for work, she put his stuff in a large box, his mug, his ties, his unread novels, his jacket, his shirt from the cleaners, his binoculars – why ever did he need binoculars? – and all the other things with which he had littered her home, so that when he returned in the evening, the box was there ready and waiting for him. What Ruth didn't want was to be cleaning up any more crumbs.

'Can't we talk about this?' said Mike. 'You're being unreasonable.'

She looked at the box. Her face softened. She looked at him. 'No,' she said.

⊱ ⊰

Strays

She had found the animal one day on her doorstep. He came as a beggar and left as a king, his hunger and curiosity well-satisfied.

'I never touch stray animals,' said her neighbour as she swept the stairs the following morning, pushing aside the empty food bowl with her slippered foot. But, in the days that followed, the woman looked on with curiosity as the cat returned and gained familiarity.

This ragged little creature entered Vivian's disordered life of aimless tasks, establishing his world of patterns and habits and rhythms within hers. When Vivian returned home at midday, she came to expect him there. Very soon he knew her routines better than she did herself. When he did not return, his absence filled Vivian with a mother's anguish. She would lean perilously over the wrought iron balcony, straining to see into obscured corners of the tangled garden below, hoping she would sight the wave of his scrawny, grey-speckled tail and hear his distant greeting.

'He'll come back,' her partner would say, though to the man it was of no importance whether he did or not. He had a vague awareness that the cat served some purpose. It gave Vivian a focus. It occupied her time in a manner he could identify. But soon he, too, was roaming the sun-baked streets, peering into shrubbery and calling out the alien name.

'So, he's got a name now,' commented her neighbour, 'but he's only a cat after all.' And, out of earshot, but as if she might be overheard through the adjoining walls, she whispered to her husband, 'Well, what do you expect? She's alone most of the time. She likes the company.' Her husband frowned, and turned the pages of his newspaper. He'd heard the shouts and the fights in the flat next door.

'Don't get involved,' he mumbled.

But his wife would do as she pleased anyway. She said nothing and went about her business, clearing plates from the table, scurrying to and fro between living room and kitchen.

Vivian grew to cherish the cat. The creaking of the huge door would signal her return and he would shoot past her, sliding along the smooth, cold surface of the tiled corridor. He had his special places in the apartment, a cushion here, a blanket there. Saucers and bowls lurked in unexpected places.

'Cats don't belong in the kitchen,' said her partner as the cat wound itself in and out of his legs. The man pushed the animal away roughly with his foot. He had important work to do, sharing out the meat just brought from the butcher's. Some was for her. The rest he would take home.

'Don't give this to the cat,' he said, reading her mind. 'It's the best cut,' and he glared in the direction of the animal, who sat – ears erect – inside a brown cardboard box in the corner of the room.

When the man left, Vivian would cook the steak, chop a section of it into small pieces and feed them one by one to the cat. It satisfied her to see the animal well-nourished, licking his paws and then stretching out his long body in the rectangle of hot sunshine that stamped itself on the beige and white tiles of her bedroom floor. Vivian lay on the bed and listened to the rare passing sounds that punctuated the silence of her room. Sometimes the cat would stay immobile for such long periods that she imagined him dead. Only when the bright geometric shape had shifted across his body and left him in too cool a shade did he resurrect himself and seek a warmer spot. Again he would stretch and roll and then view his mistress lovingly through half-closed eyes. Vivian stayed as she was, gazing absently as the shadow of the tall window frame slipped from wall to wall like a silent, confident ghost of habit. But for this sole movement, it seemed to her as though the day had a beginning, but no end. The clock would stop, and time would hover around an uncertain future. She did not know if the man would return that night or the next, or the morning that followed, or the next. It was his choice. She was his choice.

She did not know if she loved him, but she remembered that she had loved him once. Lying beside her and holding her in his arms, he would tell her that he loved her, but she thought it a strange, possessive love.

In the evenings, when she was on her own – and there were many – the cat would spring lightly onto her lap and stay there late into the night – nights when she was alone, but for the cat, and when her imagination drifted far and wide across a dark and menacing city. Together and apart, they did not belong to it, but they survived.

But then, when the man returned, the conflict and tears came too, and the muffled voices that the neighbours heard through their walls. The cat, his eyes sharp and his ears vigilant, would cower under the sofa and emerge only at the sound of his mistress's sobs and the slamming of the heavy oak door. Then, leaving tiny black footprints as he went, he would pad softly across her sheets and peer into her face. Curling close to her body in a small, round bundle, he would warm her stomach and regulate her breathing with his.

⸺⊚⸺

Vivian left one hot afternoon without any warning.

'I'm going home,' she told her neighbour, who had come to the door with an extra helping of something she had made for lunch.

'Poor dear,' the woman had said to her husband, 'she hardly eats a thing – like a breadstick she is.'

'What do you expect?' he had grunted. 'She gives it all to the cat.'

'I'm taking the five o'clock plane,' Vivian told her neighbour.

'I'm sorry,' said the woman. She had grown fond of the young foreign girl, her odd distorted pronunciation and her strange, unfamiliar manner – the way she walked and dressed, and the silent, earnest look in her eyes.

'Don't worry about the cat,' she said, anticipating Vivian's request. 'I'll watch him for you. I'll see he gets plenty to eat. We'll look after him. Don't you worry.'

Vivian packed her most precious things. The rest she left in orderly fashion in cartons of varying size. The cat watched patiently as she stored her radio and slippers and a miscellany of unread books in his old gnawed box. Then, as she trundled her suitcase along the corridor, pausing only once to look behind and assure herself that the windows were firmly closed, he hurtled past her, a grey blur disappearing down the steps and into the garden's arid undergrowth.

-->==•=) ⊂=•<--

Vivian never thought she would return, but she did. Just to make sure. The city was still violent and menacing, but it was less threatening to her now. Somehow it drew her. She was different too, though the change was difficult to define.

So her neighbour thought as she sat Vivian down in her husband's armchair. She scrutinised her — her clothes, her hair, and her expression. Less earnest, she thought.

Vivian cast her eyes along the photo frames large and small that decorated the well-polished surfaces of small tables and sideboards, reawakening memories of another world past.

'Do you still see your gentleman?' asked her neighbour as she handed across a tiny cup of inky coffee. She did not look Vivian in the eyes.

'No, not any more,' said Vivian. 'I suppose the cat died, did it?'

'Yes, I'm afraid so,' said the woman, and her face coloured slightly.

Vivian said nothing. She sipped her coffee. A coloured snapshot, its edges curled and creased, had been jammed awkwardly into the corner of a picture frame: the woman's husband smiling, holding a restless uncertain cat up towards the camera.

'Poor dear,' said the woman. 'He was knocked down by a car. He heard the door open, you see, and ran across the road to come in.' She paused and looked at Vivian. 'I'm sorry about that,' she said. 'I really am.'

'Yes, it's a shame,' said Vivian.

'Yes,' continued her neighbour, 'never mind the trouble they were — you always miss the company. It's the companionship, you see,' she said. 'That's what it is … the companionship.'

-->==•=) ⊂=•<--

Rainshine

'Is it true that you have four seasons?'

'Yes. And you?'

'We have two only. The dry season and the wet season.'

'And what is it now?'

'The wet season.'

Kate had a dream about a house, a very large house with a rain-tapped roof. She had been given an apartment of her own inside it and was excited about how she would organise herself, where she would put her things and where she would work. The apartment had cupboard space, and steps up and steps down, and doors all nicely painted in white, a pure, shiny, reflecting white. But it had no bathroom. Kate would have liked her own bathroom. That was a definite flaw, she thought.

Her part of the house was overrun with people. It was like a housewarming. They were everywhere. In and out of the rooms, to-ing and fro-ing, flowing up and flowing down, like water from a tap that had been left to run.

There was tidying up to be done. Kate remembered not being able to find the rubbish bin. She went out of the back door and turned right, though she knew she should have turned left. The bins had been moved away from the house and were lined up behind some people who were all sitting in chairs, as if in a cinema. Not a very good place to sit, she thought. Every time someone opened a bin, you got a whiff of the odour. Vile, pungent odour.

Kate thought she should take a photograph of the house. She could see it a long way off on a lovely green hill, standing in isolation, but with other buildings on other hills surrounding it. Viewing it from where she was, she realised that the main entrance was on the other side, away from her. It seemed a pity. She wondered if it was possible to build a house back-to-front, and she supposed it was.

There were other places too for the visiting, but not having the transport, she'd decided she'd be safer to stay where she was.

Kate is in the airport, waiting for her flight to Cagayan. She hopes her suitcase will turn up at the other end. She couldn't be in a strange place without her things.

The air conditioning systems are large boxes, standing like metal filing cabinets against the walls. You can hear them clattering at full blast, but they make very little difference. The heat is beginning to exhaust her. Around her, people are fanning themselves.

The names of destinations are printed in large black letters on yellow plastic boards. As each flight is called, its corresponding sign is illuminated and passengers, jostling with packages, cluster around a ground hostess, neat in navy skirt and crisp white shirt with elbow-length sleeves. People are dotted about in rows, sitting on plastic moulded seats of beiges and greens, yellows, reds and blues. A cleaner swabs methodically under and around their feet. There is a continuum of noise. Kate imagines it's like sitting in an aviary.

'Catarman, Naga, Bacolod, Iloilo, Kalibo, Legaspi, Butnan ...' These are the names she reads on the boards.

'Where are you going?' one of the girls in uniform had asked. They laughed when she couldn't pronounce the name of her destination.

Kate isn't actually sure where she is going, but she trusts that she'll arrive.

Kate dreamed that Leo had gone away, but she knew that he would be returning soon by boat at a certain port and she wanted to surprise him. When the boat arrived, she ran on board. But then she remembered that she had done nothing about her appearance. In haste, she refreshed her make-up, smoothed a little foundation on her cheeks, put on some lipstick. She was passable. Her friend Christine was there too. Kate remembered that. In the dream, she saw Leo emerge from the boat. She was excited and she rushed up to him.

He looked shocked and embarrassed. He was with other people, so she quickly made up a story to make it seem to them that she was simply an acquaintance – there was no more to it than that.

'I was just in the vicinity,' she told him. 'I knew you'd be here, so I thought I'd come along and say hello, surprise you...'

He spoke to her quietly so the others couldn't hear. 'You shouldn't have come here,' he said. 'I'm in company. Can't you see?'

As the dream progressed, he changed into someone very fat and ugly, someone quite gross. She could see Christine looking curiously at him. Kate knew what she was thinking.

'Surely that isn't the man Kate's seeing?'

So she moved away from him and she said to Christine, 'That wasn't Leo, by the way. That was just a friend of his.'

It is a bumpy, twisting road going up to Malaybalay, with wonderful jungle-like scenery of the kind Kate's only ever seen in films. Everywhere there are hills and, rising above them, mountains covered with vegetation. It is raining. She gazes out of the car window, entranced by the downpour.

'For us, rain is a blessing,' says Guia. Smiling, she adds, 'You are a blessing ... for all the teachers who are coming to learn from you.'

To their left, the far-off hills, enclosed in haze, look soft and carpeted. Close by the road there are little wooden shacks with trees bending in around them. Then there is flat land, damp farmed earth, huts with rusted, corrugated iron roofs, and everywhere glistening trees and shrubbery, and just one wet and steamy road that goes on and on. For Kate, one tree is much like the next. She wishes now that she could tell them apart. For the first time, she finds herself fascinated by nature and by what it provides. A speck of hope touches her and she thinks of renewal, the freshness of the green, transparent raindrops on leaves, clouds moving above her, shifting, stirring, revealing snatches of the palest blues and greys.

'Have you a husband?' asks Guia.

'No,' says Kate.

'No one?'

'No. No one.'

Guia turns her head for a moment to watch the rain, but then she looks back. 'Why not?' she asks.

Kate knows there are a thousand ways to answer the question. 'I'm still looking,' she says.

And Guia is easily satisfied. 'Perhaps you will find someone here.'

'Yes, perhaps,' says Kate.

They drive on. The mountains are blue in the distance. Cloud has descended over the forests, so that the light is much dimmer now. It's a journey they could never have made in the dark. There are women walking arm in arm under umbrellas, still more hills, still the same road. And here, somewhere in the middle of nowhere, they pass publicity placards, adverts for beer, warnings, greetings, welcomes. They flash past. And Kate drifts away.

In her dream, Kate followed Leo down a series of city streets. She was unfamiliar with the area, but he was walking purposefully. He seemed to know exactly where he was going. Kate hoped he wouldn't see that she was following him. He turned a corner and entered a courtyard. A child played on a brightly coloured infant's tricycle, a child with rich, dark hair, like his father's. Perhaps there was more than one child. Kate couldn't be sure. Leo bent to kiss the boy. When he stood up, he caught sight of Kate. His face was flushed.

'Why are you following me?' he said. 'You have no right. My private life is my own. You have no right to spy on me.'

'I wasn't spying,' said Kate, but she knew she was. She was there because she wanted to be part of his life and of what he had. She wanted the child too. She wanted to kiss the child and run her fingers though his hair.

A door opened and a woman stepped out. Kate could not remember what she looked like, just that she was young and very beautiful. The woman hadn't registered Kate's presence. Leo ushered the child towards his mother. He turned his back on Kate and entered the house. She was still standing there in the empty courtyard when he closed the door behind him.

Kate sees Grace and Guia strolling about in the sun under a large black umbrella, and she finds it odd. They wave to her as they cross the corner of the campus, passing from light to dark, disappearing into the shade. The sun is harsh, the heat oppressive and sticky. In Kate's hotel room there is an electric fan. It rattles like an old train and keeps her awake at night. Her legs are bitten and sore. She lies on the bed rubbing her fingers over the itchy bumps. She is angry with herself, for her lack of ease, for her inability to adapt.

The teachers are getting used to her. They sit before her now in rows, wanting to know about her country and her way of life. Simple questions with simple answers that she thinks they might not care to hear. But they do. They care very much.

'And, in December, it snows?'

'Sometimes,' she says, 'but usually later ... if it does at all.' She asks them if they've ever seen snow.

'Only on television,' they tell her, 'and in pictures.'

She talks. She explains. The work drains her. She isn't at all sure how much the teachers know or how much they really understand. Some faces are alert, smiling constantly; other teachers, she sees, are dozing. Their eyes close wearily as her voice drones on in this foreign language of hers. It goes well nonetheless, but she has her private superstitions. She tries not think too much of herself lest fate will rob her.

The teachers are keen to chat in the breaks, telling her about delicacies from their towns and villages. Kate, who has always rationed herself in the company of others, takes time to sit and talk, answering their questions about what she thinks of the place and the people and the food, and where she has been, and where she is going.

Guia, Elvira, Grace and the others bring her foods to sample. She likes the desserts and learns the names: sweets made of rice... *puto*, *suman*, *biko*. She tells them that *biko* is like the rice puddings her grandmother used to make. From long ago she remembers her grandmother in the kitchen in her stained apron, stooping to lift the puddings from the oven in their brown earthenware dishes. There was always something special waiting for Kate when she came home, always something to look forward to.

Kate had the strangest of dreams. She and Leo were in a pleasant sort of place – she didn't know where – walking about, shaded from the rainshine by a large umbrella. She had this knowledge that he was married. Not that he had told her. She just knew. They were talking and then at some point during their conversation, he slipped in some comments about 'my wife.' He didn't call her by name, just 'my wife.' Kate had the impression he wanted her to acknowledge what he had said. She didn't, but in her dream she was profoundly sorrowful. In the back of her dream-mind she thought, 'That's it. I'll never have him now,' and she had a sense of extreme loss. Leo's hands were tanned and he wore a gold ring on his wedding finger. And Kate knew that when he took the ring off there would be a pale mark on his hand, an outline of where it had been.

The teachers can read Kate's mind. Whenever she thinks of something, it appears. A book, a pen, a postcard, a glass of water. She thinks of a meal and it appears. Respecting her privacy they bring the food to her: breakfast in her room in the morning, lunch at a meeting table in the principal's office. She always eats alone, but then it's nothing new, being alone. She eats dinner at six in her hotel room. It's like being under house arrest, but where else would she want to go? It rains every night and, when it rains, the lights go out and the streets are enveloped in darkness. Kate is trapped alone in the dark with her thoughts.

An older teacher comes to her during one of the breaks. She has the sort of sad, watery eyes that make her look as though she has been weeping. Her name is Teresita. She wants to show Kate photos of her husband when he was studying abroad. They are black and white photographs – all different sizes. The first is of a slim young man with a smooth, handsome face. He is standing outside a smart suburban house.

'He went on a scholarship,' says Teresita. The date is written on the reverse of the photo. 1964. There are more photos ... in Reading, in Stratford, in Oxford and then, surprisingly, Paris. The date on the last photograph is 1968. The man looks changed. He wears sunglasses. He is smartly dressed. He is detached and superior.

'He's away now,' says Teresita. 'He's travelling.'

Kate stares at the photo, looking for clues to the man's secret world.

Kate had a memory, unearthed like a photo from the past. Before Leo there had been Roberto. In her mind's eye, the two men merged, one superimposed over the other. Roberto became Leo, and Leo Roberto. Past became present, and present past.

There was one day from the past that she could not erase. When her thoughts wandered, she replayed that scene many times. She saw herself as she had been that day, hysterical, out of control, tears streaking her cheeks. She was alone in the house where Roberto had left her after telling her about the child. It had been so easy for him just to tell her and leave, knowing that when he returned she would be there waiting for him.

She ran from the apartment onto the terrace from where she could see Roberto in the street below her about to unlock his car. She screamed at him.

'You bastard!' she screamed. 'You bastard!' He looked up terrorised, more from fear of who might hear than of Kate herself. She saw the alarm in his face and she screamed louder ... obscenities ... anything she could think of in her language and in his ... anything that would make him take notice. There was no one to hear her. Only him. The surrounding villas were uninhabited in the winter and she was living in isolation. She came indoors and sank in a heap on the floor. She pressed her face against the wall and wept.

'You bastard,' she cried, as if that would make a difference. He had wanted her there. She had made sacrifices for him. She had travelled to be with him.

She heard his key in the door and then he was there by her side, taking her in his arms, stroking her hair and wiping the tears from her face.

'How can you blame a baby?' he was saying. 'When you see them, you realise.' What he said made little sense to her. He spoke haltingly. 'The children. They're helpless. We're responsible. We bring them into the world. They've no say in the matter.'

She bit her lip. Why could she not tell him she blamed him? Why could she not speak her mind? He had told her the baby was due soon. He said he hadn't known. He hadn't known his wife was pregnant until quite late.

'I didn't know how to tell you,' he said. 'I didn't want you not to come. This won't change anything. It'll still be the same between us.'

She looked at him, and her eyes smarted as she looked. She had wanted him for her. She had trusted him. She wondered how he could betray her now and expect things not to change. In her heart, she cursed his baby. She wished it dead.

It starts to rain. The water comes in torrents.

'The lights will go out soon,' she thinks and then there is a chorus of dismayed voices from outside. Her fan spins to a halt and heat envelopes her. Another evening in darkness. People scramble about, finding and lighting candles. Lights flicker and she opens her blind to let in some of that faint illumination, but she sees nothing from her window. Downstairs, reading by the light of a hurricane lamp, she notices something scurry past the feet of the receptionist. Kate is unprepared for things that lurk in the dark.

Kate dreamed that her mother was there and that she had to tell her that she was dead. Her mother didn't know yet that she was supposed to be dead and she was carrying on as normal.

'You're not supposed to be here,' Kate told her. 'You're dead.'

'Am I?' said her mother, and seemed a bit perplexed.

Then she dreamt that her mother actually was dead and she had come back, appearing to her as a ghostly apparition. Kate was struck through with terror. She put her head under the bedclothes and screamed. She called out for Leo. She saw him in the distance, standing immobile. She continued to call his name, until she saw him close up. Only then did she feel consoled and relieved, as though everything would be all right. There was no need to be afraid. She was safe because he was there. She had put her trust in him.

She wakes damp with perspiration, as she has done at other times through the nights. There is always noise ... cats wail, dogs howl, cocks crow, rusty old mopeds grind past, rattling and blasting. That night, compared to the others, has been quiet. A group of women pass in procession under her window. They are chanting Hail Marys. She looks at her watch. It is five in the morning.

The images were still fresh in her memory. She could see his window from where she was parked across the street. It was distantly illuminated like a large television set in a darkened room. She had cut short a trip and returned late that evening, picking up her car at the station. It was an unusually humid summer's night. She'd had an intense desire to see him. They had argued but now she regretted her abruptness of the day before. Over the phone, Leo had sounded curt – diffident. It was her fault – she knew that, but she was there now to make amends. She wondered if she should go up to his flat right away or phone beforehand.

Leo's figure came into sight at the window. He wore a white shirt, open at the collar. His hair appeared ruffled. He was bowed, pouring himself a drink. He looked up and for a moment he remained framed in the window, staring out in her direction, fixing the space beyond in half recognition. For all the strangeness of this gesture, Kate could not be sure he had seen her. She turned slightly to open the car door, watching the frame pulsate before her eyes in the darkness, and, as she watched, her movements slowed and the moment was held in time.

A girl – a small, vivacious, dark-haired girl – had entered the frame. Kate observed the picture as in an art gallery, a tableau. A young woman and Leo in the frame together, the two playing and joking, embracing each other, but Leo still looking out over her shoulder towards the window, searching in the darkness for some familiar, spying face. He took the girl firmly by the shoulders and pulled her to him out of sight. They were gone. Kate started up the engine and drove on.

The teachers are showing Kate pictures of their families, their children.

'Just the one?' she asks Guia.

'Yes,' says Guia, 'just one.' Kate has a sense that Guia understands something about her. Kate knows this, but she has no idea why. She examines the other photographs.

There are tiny children on beaches, sitting under palm trees with their fathers. There are babies with soft round faces and tightly closed eyes. There are babies enveloped in blankets in their mothers' arms. Joji has two babies.

'You look too young,' says Kate, and Joji and the others laugh at the joke. They all look too young for such wisdom.

'And you have no children?' asks Zenie, as the others have before her. Kate shakes her head and smiles.

'We are so sorry,' says Apple. She speaks the thoughts of her colleagues.

Guia puts her arm around Kate and hugs her.

'You are beautiful,' says Grace, and the teachers nod their dark heads in agreement.

Kate and Christine sat together in silence on the carpet in front of the fire. Kate was pouring the tea.

'What did she have?' asked Christine.

'A boy,' said Kate.

'And he didn't tell you?' said Christine after a long pause.

'No,' said Kate.

Christine looked down into her cup. Kate guessed she was stopping herself from saying what she wanted to say. That she blamed her friend for not having seen the situation as it was. When Christine looked up, tears were rolling down Kate's face.

'I know,' said Christine. 'I know. You wanted it to be your child. You wanted Roberto to give you his child.'

'Yes,' said Kate. Her voice was halting. 'I almost thought ...' She found it difficult to put the words together. 'I thought,' she said, 'that I wasn't good enough.'

Guia can't come to the final morning of the workshop. She gives Kate an envelope, a thank-you letter, and she apologises.

'It's like I worked to prepare a party,' she says, 'and then I get sick at the last minute.'

Kate is sorry and takes Guia's hand in hers. 'I'll miss you,' she says.

Elvira takes their photograph together. They exchange addresses. Guia embraces Kate. Her frame is small and wiry in Kate's arms.

'Salamat gid!' she says. 'I thank you very much. I will not forget you and the learnings I got these past days.'

Kate is embarrassed. She has done nothing of any significance that she can remember.

'I wish,' says Guia, 'I wish one day you can come again to us.'

Kate puts Guia's letter in her bag. She will read it later, she says.

Guia's letter lies among the things the women have given her, the bright red and blue necklace made from the tiniest of beads, batik cloths in brown and maroon and ochre, a certificate of appreciation, and postcards carrying blessings and obscure addresses. Kate is far from her friends now, and their voices are only in her head. She misses them, though she never imagined she would. She looks again at these things and she reaches for the letter. It is time for dinner and tomorrow she has an early departure. She replaces the letter, picks up her key and goes to the door. Guia's letter lies on the bed unopened. It is of little importance. But Kate returns to look at it.

Guia's husband went to see their child after it was born.

'The baby is not so well,' the doctor had told him as she led him into the room with its machines and wires and tubes.

'We'll baptise him now,' he told Guia when he came back, and then he cried. Guia stroked his cheek and wiped away his tears. She knew her baby would be well.

'He will be better soon,' she told her husband, 'and then we will all go home together.'

Guia knew nothing could happen to her baby. She said so as she leaned over his cot and touched his motionless fingers. Her mother-in-law brought her a chair and made her sit down.

'God will make my baby well,' Guia told her. She was sure of it. Her mother-in-law nodded and held Guia's hand.

Guia went to mass that afternoon in the hospital chapel. The priest told of a child who had died but was raised from the dead.

'If God can bring the dead back to life,' she thought, 'then He can surely make my baby well. It is not asking too much of Him.'

Guia sat by her baby's side and spoke to him ... about his toys waiting to be played with at home ... about the clothes they had made for him and the cabinet his father had built for his things.

'Everyone is waiting for you,' she told him. 'You must get better fast so we can go home.' She had always talked to him. She had talked to him when she had carried him inside her.

'Show me that you understand what I'm telling you,' she would say, and she would feel his kicks in response.

'Show me that you understand me now,' she said. And he did. He moved, clutching silently at the air.

The doctor came to Guia early the following morning. She and her husband were having breakfast. The doctor spoke softly and slowly and, as she did, she drew a horizontal line in the air with her finger.

The teachers had been exchanging stories, Kate remembers. It was the story of the gardener and his rose that she liked best.

'The gardener had a rose plant,' said Guia, 'which he favoured above all others.' The women moved closer to hear her story. Guia continued.

'He took extra special care of it, because he wanted to give that flower to his master. One day, to his dismay, he discovered that someone has picked the rose.' Guia's delicate fingers plucked at the air, and here the teachers sighed. 'And he was so sad,' said Guia. 'The master,' she said, 'he sensed the gardener's mood. He asked him, "What is wrong?"'

The teachers were quite silent. They waited.

'The gardener told him,' said Guia, her eyes wide now upon her audience. 'And the master said ...' And here she paused. 'And the master said ... that he himself has picked the rose because he too – like the gardener – has favoured that rose amongst all the others.'

The teachers clapped and then resumed their chatter. Guia turned to look at Kate and smiled.

'And I thank Him,' writes Guia, 'for lending us our son.'

Kate puts down the letter and smooths its pages in front of her on the bed. 'For lending us our son,' reads Kate. She has read it many times now. The whole letter. She relives – plays back – her conversations with Guia. She reinterprets them, or tries to, in the light of what she knows now. She thinks of things said between them. Things she said or might have said, ideas that might have had another meaning for her friend, a meaning not intended for the mother of a lost child.

Kate has an early departure in the morning and it is late. She has not been to dinner. The dim, fluctuating light of the hotel room has hurt her eyes. She goes to the bathroom where the light is stronger and she looks at her face in the mirror. She looks to see if she has changed. And she weeps now as bitterly and as intensely as the day she cursed Roberto's baby.

'This is Leo speaking.' On the answering machine, his voice has a slow, stilted tone. 'I am calling from ...'

Kate is sitting with her photographs spread in front of her. Molecules of dust float downwards to their surface in a spotlight of sunshine. It has been a long time.

'Perhaps we can meet ...' His voice is hesitant. He leaves his number – a new number. There is sunshine after the morning's rain, but the air is not humid here. Kate looks at the photographs as she listens. The message ends. Kate erases the message.

In her final week, they took her to the monastery of the Transfiguration, chauffeured by the principal's driver. They saw the buildings a long way off, standing in isolation on a rich green hill.

'It's raining,' chanted Elvira, though the earth was drier here.

'Have you seen the fruit tree of the mango?' asked Grace. Kate hadn't. They each scanned the passing landscape for one to show her.

'Here, look. Here is mango tree,' said Elvira pointing and pulling at Kate's sleeve.

'And bananas,' said Guia.

'You don't have like this at home,' said Grace.

'They just grow,' said Elvira.

'Even if you don't plant them,' said Guia, and the car bumped and lurched up the hill's stony path.

At the top, they bundled Kate out. Grace chattered, Elvira guided and carried the camera. Guia looped her arm in Kate's. The sun was shining weakly after the downpour. Inside the building, they were silenced and became reverent. The monks were chanting a Benediction.

'Perhaps it will rain again,' whispered Elvira. The clouds were smudged and brown on the horizon. Kate didn't care if it rained now and washed away the grime. A white-robed monk led them down concrete steps and onto a wide terrace from where they could see the roughly-built outhouses and the static grey of the rice fields.

'Here is guava tree,' said Elvira triumphantly, pointing into dense, olive-coloured vegetation. They took a photo against a leafy backcloth. Kate and Guia, Guia and Elvira. Many permutations.

They followed the monk up more stairs and along external passageways, fenced by green-painted railings. They passed the refectory, with all the places set in orderly fashion for the men's supper. They turned then to face the forests, stretching far before them, a vast rich sparkling green, a horizon overrun with trees and, above the trees, a violent and confused sky, shot through with an intense spectrum of light.

The women were ecstatic.

'Can you see it?' they cried.

'Look,' said Elvira, 'not one rainbow, but two.'

'It is a blessing,' proclaimed the monk, laughing and welcoming the sight with a wave of his arm. 'You are blessed,' he said. 'You have brought us rain.'

'And shine,' said Guia.

Kate couldn't see it at first.

'Yes, yes,' said Grace. 'Look here,' she said, holding Kate by the shoulders and shifting her into position.

'Here,' said Guia. And taking Kate's arm, she pointed it up towards the sky and, holding Kate's finger lightly in her hand, she traced the shape of the second rainbow in the air.

Kate gazed into the sky, now following the rainbows as they arched elegantly towards the clouds and then curved downwards. Like magic arrows through the rainshine.

⊷▦ ▦⊷

Charmed

Through the holiday, Tess had become accustomed to expecting Sunni's attention, but she now found he was dispensing it meanly. It grieved her these last few days when he said he could not come with her on the morning horse rides. She was not at all sure if the hotel staff or the grooms down at the stables had noticed her interest so she looked for confirmation in their faces. If they knew anything, they gave no indication. Well, that's what they were paid for, after all. As for Sunni, he had phone calls to make, people to see, workmen to supervise, and he had to say his prayers.

Perhaps Sunni saw her only as his one out-of-season tourist, and fair game at that. In intimacy, his message was clear. By the light of day, it had come to spell a warning of caution or simply a lack of interest. She was not sure which. She gathered that it was permissible for her to ride alone into the parklands with just the groom, but not with him, not with Sunni. She could not measure him on her terms and it frustrated her. There would have been some satisfaction in protesting, but she did not. She knew better than that.

This place with its ragged farmlands and its makeshift habitations isolated her from the thin air, the greyishness, the damp orderliness of home, all paused in her mind's eye – buildings, cars, subways, cafes. The blast of her city traffic muffled into Indian birdsong. Here there were no roads, no pavements, no coffee queues, no raincoats. There were narrow tracks, and shrubbery snug with surprises: little brown-faced children with skeletal arms and blue-black hair; wizened old hags with bare, crinkled midriffs, bent under huge bundles of twiggish branches; flea-bitten buffalo herded by girls, waif-like and sullen, swathed in their mothers' red-dyed cottons.

That day before her departure, it was different. When she came for her ride, three horses – not two – were saddled. She understood there was a plan of sorts. Sunni was in the stable yard taking his tea in silence and smoking a cigarette while the men squatted around him in the sand, relating to him the business of the coming day. When he was done, he stood up and, giving her only the briefest of glances, said, 'Shall we go?'

Riding partly on the dirt track and partly on the grassy banks, they cleared the encampment, picking their way through a miscellany of sheep and dogs, and a crowd of grubby infants that ran alongside them squealing at the sight of the horses. Sunni always rode the new and most skittish mares. Tess rode directly behind him while Bhanji, the dark-skinned groom, trailed them at a distance. From time to time, Sunni's horse nose-dived or leapt, and once or twice its hooves spat dirt into her face.

'Not so close,' he called, half turning and spreading one hand towards her as he rode. 'Or you'll be coming with no teeth.'

As he pushed his horse forward, his good humour restored, she heard him chuckle. Keeping her head down, clear of the low branches, she watched him, observing the ease with which his body balanced the movement of the animal. She asked herself how a man – this man – could align his passions with belief in his gods, how he could pray in all sincerity, and then love illicitly.

He led her out beneath the hills into a vast field of shoulder-high corn. It seemed impenetrable, but then she saw that it was burrowed through with snake-thin paths. The air was humid and she was thankful for the flood of breeze rushing past her ears, drying the perspiration that mottled her brow. Bhanji rustled past her on his horse and took the lead. Sunni fell in behind him as he made his way through the bristling stalks. Slowing his horse, Bhanji looked around him as though in doubt. The two men paused, exchanged a rapid burst of words. Then the groom turned his horse and retraced his steps, brushing past her again, leather against leather. Sunni stayed at the rear. She turned to look at him.

'Where are we going?'

'A special place. You'll see.' He waved her on.

They continued at a walk, pushing aside the stiff dry crops, trampling them underfoot.

After ten minutes or so they came to a grassy clearing, grazed by a pair of goats. Five, perhaps six, children stood immobile and staring. Behind them, a jerry-built mud structure with a rough dirt-covered courtyard just visible from the outside. Bhanji was already on the ground, taking the reins of the young mare as Sunni dismounted. Tess slid down from her saddle and followed at a distance, wary of being an object of curiosity. An ancient, bespectacled man, draped in soiled white cloth and with legs like bamboo, shuffled forward and bent, with one arm outstretched, to touch Sunni's feet. Sunni stopped him before he could topple. He chattered at the man then placed his palms together in greeting. The man reciprocated, but with humility, with reverence.

Water was brought to them on a tin tray, carried out from the enclosure by a small boy. Tess reached for one of the glasses.

'Don't drink,' said Sunni.

'No?' she said.

'No.'

He called to Bhanji to bring the bottled water from his saddlebag. And when the bottle arrived, he said, 'This is yours.'

All along he kept up a lively banter with the old man, and with several generations of his family, who were gradually assembling around them. Then came the hot, sweet Masala tea, brought to them in tarnished aluminium beakers.

'This you can drink.'

The old man sipped his tea and sucked at the flattened end of a cigarette. He studied Tess and directed at Sunni what could only have been questions about her.

'He wants to know if you are married and how many children you have.'

'Surely he knows,' said Tess.

Sunni translated. The man laughed out loud, his bony shoulders juddering up and down. He jabbered back a response.

'He will help you,' said Sunni.

'Do I need help?' said Tess.

'He thinks so.'

He and the old man spoke again. 'What is your problem,' said Sunni, 'he will give you magic to fix it.'

'I don't mind being fixed.'

'He can cure cattle of snake bites. I've seen it. He has a power.'

'And city snakes – can he cure those?'

The old man creaked to his feet supported by one of his numerous daughters.

'Go inside,' said Sunni, 'but take off your boots.' He laughed. 'And your socks.'

She gave him a look.

'Go on,' he said.

She approached the house and, leaning against the wall, she wriggled first out of one boot and then the other. She peeled off her socks and wondered at the forgotten whiteness of her feet. The children stood at a distance whispering.

'Right foot first.'

She turned slightly. 'Are you coming?'

'Not allowed.' He narrowed his eyes and took a long drag of his cigarette. 'Go on,' he repeated.

She stepped over the threshold right foot first. At the entrance, the old man poured water into her hands from a silver-coloured pitcher. He ushered her into what looked like a tiny shrine and indicated that she should sit opposite him on the ant-infested ground. Pictures lined the walls around them, symbols, images of gods and goddesses, some cut from newspapers or magazines. All kinds of paraphernalia littered the altar, or what passed for an altar.

This talk of snakes had propelled her back. When she returned – and she would have to return – nothing would be altered. One strange and mystical world was temporary; the other was permanent. Soon this world of the horses, the land, of nature's busy silence, and of him, would be memory only, images remembered. She could change her location but not her reality. Her snakes would be as before, poisoning the work she loved, making each day a sufferance, sabotaging her every decision. Being away gave her the illusion of it not existing. Her troubles would not go away; they would wait for her to come back. She needed the courage to make it stop, magic if it came to that, a cure for snake bites. She had drawn a line under the limits of her tolerance.

The old man took out a ball of red wool, like the unravelled yarn of someone's old jumper. He took the end of the strand and ran it between his toes. He measured a length, which he broke off and then entwined around his fingers. From a blackened sheet of rolled newspaper he took two sticks of dun-coloured incense. After two or three tries he lit them with a tiny match.

As the fragrance wafted up between them, he chanted, holding the wool over the incense cloud. He twirled and twisted the yarn. Then, as he spoke incantations, he wove knots into it.

Perhaps she should have wished not for immunity or protection, but for love. Not just that she might be loved, but that she herself might love. Would she then prioritize work before love? Work was real. Love was imaginary. That's how she saw it. As for the others, would they know, she wondered, that in this precise moment a spell had been cast that flew in their direction? She was charmed, but they were damned. There was at least some pleasure in believing this.

At the entrance to the enclosure, Bhanji had approached, curious to watch the proceedings. The old man looked up brusquely from his work and barked a warning at him. The man retreated. The incantation was private and was for her only.

The realisation came to her then that this was her chance, this was her time, and that she should indeed have wished for a love spell to be put on the one she most desired.

Or else in time he would be lost.

⊱⊰

And the past fades like our dreams. Had it been so long since that day? Six years, or was it seven?

From the veranda, Tess could see the foothills shaded green and purple in the distance. In the forecourt, two tour buses stood with their engines humming. Soon the lunchtime visitors from Jodhpur would file back on board and consult their guidebooks about the next destination. Tess sat in her usual place at the marble-topped table, a glass of rum in front of her. On her many visits to the hotel, she had noted few changes. A coat of paint here and there, some rooms refurbished, horses sold on and new ones purchased. The staff were the same. She knew all their names and they knew about her. The changes were for the most part in herself. Her confidence, her achievements. She could measure her success in terms of financial security, in terms of having the power of the last word, of being the one who signed off on projects, and the one who hired and fired.

An unfurled blind flapped gently behind her. The jarring call of the peacocks rose from the gardens. Sunni was the same. She regarded him as he sat in silence reading his newspaper.

'Where did you go this morning?' she asked.

He looked up and reached for his cigarettes. 'To the old man's farm.'

'Old man?' she said.

'The medicine man.' He looked beyond her.

'He's still alive then? I'd like to see him again.'

Sunni lit his cigarette and said nothing as though he had not heard or did not care to hear. Moments passed and then he said, 'You don't believe that nonsense?'

'I might,' she said.

He gave a snort.

'Who did you go with?' she said.

'Bhanji,' he said, 'and one of the French riders.' With a brief nod he indicated towards the archway.

She turned and followed his gaze. A young blonde woman approached. They exchanged smiles. The girl was fresh from the shower. Her hair hung damp around her neck. Rising to his feet, Sunni called to her.

'Stand over here,' he said. The girl moved towards him. A knotted red string drooped around her upper arm. 'What a mess you've made!' He was chuckling. When she was close, Sunni released the knot and unravelled the yarn.

'You have to face north,' he said.

'Why north?' said the girl, smoothing a strand of hair from her brow.

'You always face north.'

And Tess thought, 'Yes, you always face north.' He had told her that.

With both hands, Sunni gripped the girl's slim, bare arms and turned her around. Then he drew the string around her right arm and knotted it firmly. The girl looked down at his hands as they worked.

'There,' he said.

They looked directly into each other's eyes. He spun her around. He gleamed with new charm. 'Now it will work,' he said.

'Will it?' said the girl.

'Oh yes,' said Tess, 'I tried it, and it worked for me.'

⸭⟶◉ ◉⟵⸭

The Finger of Advice

THERE IS A very simple reason why some fathers – many fathers, perhaps – try to sabotage their daughters' acquisition of a boyfriend. They – the fathers – were once boyfriends themselves. They remember very well their own transgressions.

Isabel cast her mind back to a very early boyfriend whose name was Nicholas. For his age, Nicholas was the ultimate in diplomacy when it came to dealing with fathers. He was very proper, law-abiding, respectful, tidy, cultured, well-spoken, well-educated, well-attired, well ... everything, though not necessarily all in that order. And, in the presence of parents, fathers in particular, he said the right things at the right time. He was a 'Yes, Sir. Absolutely not, Sir,' kind of person.

Coming as he did from a well-to-do family that lived in an equally well-to-do part of the city, he had access to the elegant homes and the enviable vehicles of others. He would turn up on dates in MGs, or even Lamborghinis. Lucky Isabel! They were once stopped for speeding down Piccadilly from Oxford Circus, but Nicholas was so charming to the policeman that he was let off with the lightest of warnings. Isabel thought him quite brilliant. Others might have thought him either very smart or a total liability.

One Sunday afternoon, Nicholas joined Isabel and her family at home in the formal guise of a prospective boyfriend. Since a cousin of Isabel's was present, together with a suitor of her own, Isabel's father took the opportunity to expound on the subject of trust and responsibility. Listening between the lines as it were, Isabel gathered that he was really telling them that boyfriends of any sort were untrustworthy. They played along, knowing that when his discourse was concluded, they would be free to go.

'It's like this,' said her father, proffering a finger. 'You give them a finger …' For "them," he intended "boyfriends," '… and they take the whole hand.' He looked very pleased with himself. This was, of course, in the days when "giving someone the finger," was not in people's everyday verbal repertoire.

Isabel had never before thought of this finger and hand analogy. It was quite clever of him to put it that way, but did he really think they would believe him? Perhaps it would be the girlfriend who would start by having just a finger and then taking the boyfriend for his whole hand.

With the parable, or metaphor – or whatever it was supposed to be – over and, certain that they would be affected by his meaning, Isabel's father let them go for their walk in the park, having secured their promise to be back by tea-time.

Outside, the four of them squeezed into a silver Porsche, property of Nicholas's neighbour, the son of a prominent West End jeweller. From Central London they drove, with hood down and hair flowing to Windsor, where they did a tour of the castle, bought themselves ice-creams, fed the pigeons, and watched the changing of the guard. What a lovely afternoon it was. Then, they got back into the car, and Nicholas's foot on the accelerator got them back home for tea-time.

'How was the park?' said Isabel's father.

'Lovely,' said Isabel. 'We bought ice-creams and fed the birds.'

⊷═○ ○═⊶

The Writing of Wrongs

Louise.

LOUISE HAD DETERMINED that she would destroy the man for what he had done. As she saw it, 'destroy' was neither too harsh nor too violent a word. It was exactly what she had intended to do and she near enough had.

'He'll see,' she thought. 'He'll get what he deserves.'

⊷▬▭ ▭▬⊶

And now he was hers. Totally.

'A spoonful of commitment is worth precious little,' thought Louise.

She had wanted all of him. Now, as she had wished him to be, he was drawn to her magnetically, distressed on every occasion when she distanced herself from him, longing in her absence for her physical presence, for the reassurance of her words, for that strength of mind and thought that he could no longer find within himself. Strong he may have been, but now Louise had 'destroyed' him.

'Good,' thought Louise. 'Let's kick the bastard when he's down.'

⊷▬▭ ▭▬⊶

Stefan.

Stefan did not know that it was Louise's doing.

'What's happening?' he had asked himself, and spread a white beard of shaving cream across the prickly surface of his chin.

'What's wrong?' he repeated. 'It can't be me.'

He had attributed his mishaps to external circumstances, events beyond his control. Their accumulation had caused a landslide within the future he had constructed for himself, his career and his private life. The one affected the other. Stefan had been like a child trying to run with his shoelaces tied ... both legs cheated him and brought him crashing. Now he cried on the inside and acted normally on the outside. Stefan was like that, but then perhaps all men are.

⊷▬◉ ◉▬⊶

Louise had looked on confidently, smugly even. Stefan had caused her much pain, and she had returned that pain in the only way she knew how, through her deceit, her calculation, her cunning.

'My mind can equal yours,' she had said to herself as she lay in bed at night, thinking of the humiliations she had suffered because of him. Her mind could equal his, and it did.

⊷▬◉ ◉▬⊶

Louise and Stefan. This was their story.

Two minds in combat. An invisible war. For no particular reason except for the protection of egos and the saving of face. Was Louise the villain of this piece? Possibly. It had been a long and complex battle. For every strategy of his, she had a counter strategy. Stefan was an intelligent man. Louise was surprised and challenged by his intelligence.

'Smart move,' she'd think, and she'd wonder how he had anticipated her words or actions. At times she had felt she could not measure up. Stefan was always one step ahead and that was why he had managed to hurt her.

In effect, their battle was a subtle one. She never admitted to him that they were at war. He never admitted to her that he had taken up the gauntlet. Louise's power was her persistence. If she had been a rat, she would have been the last rat hanging on to the sinking ship. She would have climbed back on, bedraggled and exhausted to claim her territory and sail away triumphant.

'I'll win in the end,' she had thought.

Stefan did not have this quality. Essentially, he was weak and Louise knew she would discover him to be weak if she waited long enough and took action for long enough. She had the patience. Louise's resolute patience was her power.

'I'm a woman,' she thought. 'It's what I do best.' She would have liked to tell other women that they too had a secret weapon. She would have trained them in its use.

'Men won't know what's hit them,' she thought.

Louise was weak when she was uncertain, when she unsure of Stefan's breaking point. She was weak – she *had* been weak, and she regretted it – in her loneliness, and Stefan had found her in her loneliness. Stefan's words, his touch, his lips on hers, his tongue reaching for hers. Ah, Stefan! These things had brought about her near downfall. She could see it now. She squirmed with private embarrassment and disbelief at her own naivety, and she buried her head in her pillow at the thought.

'How could you?' she thought. 'How could you?' But she wasn't sure if it was Stefan or herself that she blamed more.

Louise's life had been focused before that first moment she and Stefan had shared.

'A man like this,' she had thought, 'so successful, so handsome, so ... influential. Why should he want me?'

⁂

He did not. No, not at all. Louise, you were right. What did *he* care?

⁂

Jennifer. She merits half a mention.

Stefan wanted Jennifer. Stefan *had* Jennifer. He'd already spent eight years of his life with her. Why should he change now? Stefan wanted Jennifer because she gave him security, because she ironed his shirts and tidied his home – 'Have you seen those socks, Jennifer?' – because she prepared his meals – 'Too much salt, Jennifer' – and engaged his guests in intelligent conversation – 'Leave the professor to me, Jennifer' — a charming hostess at his dinner parties, a tiny beautiful creature to accompany him to conferences and faculty parties, like an expensive cat on a lead. Stefan wanted to keep Jennifer because she gave him adequate satisfaction, sufficient praise and occasional passion.

'Things are just fine,' thought Stefan. 'This is the way I like it.'

*

Stefan had wanted two women ... or more.

'Things are going well,' he used to say to himself, smoothing his hand down along the length of his eau-de-cologned neck and appreciating his strong heroic profile in the bathroom mirror. Having achieved two, he could afford to take risks with others. Not in such a way that his reputation might be jeopardised, for he would break loose and fly at the slightest inkling of a threat to his work or his home.

'This is getting too heavy,' he would say. 'Time to move on.'

Stefan did not want what he could have, what was given freely. Stefan wanted only what he could *not* have so that he could make it his own, claim it as a trophy. Once captured, his prey was of no further value other than for idle play. It was in this way that Stefan was the cause of Louise's pain. By leading her to believe in him, by promising love through his words and gestures, by loving her physically, and then casting her away. Stefan, you see, would scribble on Louise's heart and then tear it up and throw it in his waste bin.

In the bin you go, Louise. In the bin you go.

*

For Louise, not seeing Stefan, not hearing him, waiting in uncertainty for his call, was indescribable and absurd torment.

'Call, won't you? Please call me,' she begged him in her mind.

She dared not mention it even to her closest friends. She feared their ridicule and their incredulity.

Ah, Louise, just another unheard voice in the arid desert of infatuation.

The love Louise offered returned as a pain within her body that spread to her brain. Louise's thoughts had wandered and lost their way. Her work, which had been her reason for existing, suffered as she suffered. Yet, when she rallied and succeeded in telling herself she could win back her mind, Stefan took it from her like a jealous child.

Louise recreated and re-lived Stefan in her mind. She remembered his touch, her touch, and his ecstasy. Only him. The reality of these thoughts sent waves of craving and wanting through her body and mind. Her waking hours all consumed in this desire for him, to have him, to be in him, to know his mind, to touch with the tips of her fingers, to caress, to lick and to savour his bodily fluids.

'Like this,' she thought. 'This is how I want you. This is the way you must be.' In her waiting days – long days into nights and nights into days – she thought only of this.

'Why don't you call me?' she would say.

When Louise had reassembled herself, Stefan was ready to take from her again. Returning, it was time for him to satisfy his ego, to reward both mind and body for the labours of those weeks away.

'I got back last week,' he'd say. 'I've been so busy. You've no idea. Perhaps we can meet? A quick drink.' It was more than that, of course. Louise wanted it to be, but it was never quite as she imagined it.

⫘ ⫘

Stefan tested her. He sought the limits of her degradation. He employed her to bring him almost, but not quite, to the point of his ecstasy. Then, with an excuse he would dismiss her to return desirous to Jennifer, and to revel in silent fantasies of women's lips and kisses on his limbs.

'I have to go now,' he would say. 'It's getting late.'

And before Louise knew it, he was gone.

Louise was Stefan's victim for a long time, existing as an accessory within his world of dreams. She was manipulated by him for longer in her perception than she was in her reality, but Stefan drained her nonetheless.

And then she fought back.

It happens to us all at some point in our lives. Let's be honest. Louise had been sliding down an iceberg into a black, icy abyss, knowing that she must find a foothold.

Think about it. This is life, not melodrama. Louise was torn on the sharp, glassy surface. She was cold and injured, plummeting beyond human return. She knew it could not be *her* slithering past the mirror. She was not to be the victim, not meant to be. Something inside Louise, that had always been inside her and had made her the person she was, was trying to save her. It obstructed her descent.

'That's enough of that,' it was saying. 'It's happened once too often.'

She knew it had. She caught her breath. She won back her mind – momentarily – during one of Stefan's neglects of her. He, confident that she was in his power; she, awakened from his trance, though still desirous of him, but as she wanted him, not as he wanted himself to be for himself.

The tunnel had righted itself. The long, dark, spinning tunnel, the one you fall into when you're like Louise. It was before her now. The path was obvious, and yet it had not before identified itself to her. Stefan's contacts, his colleagues, his associates were hers too. His influence was hers.

This was the way. It was clear to Louise now. A word here, a whisper there, a hint... just an indication.

'I hate to mention it,' she would begin. 'It's something I have to tell you,' she would say. 'It's important you should know now, before others come to hear of it ...'

A mention of unreliability, unprofessional behaviour, unacceptable practices, worse still, talk of plagiarism, the taking from others and making it one's own.

'Personally,' she would add, 'I wouldn't want to be associated with him. I'm sure you wouldn't want to risk your ... your reputation ...'

And when Louise had done all this, when she had spread the word and yet had not, having not been responsible, having only suggested or intimated. When she had done all this, Stefan's climate changed. His sunny days grew pale, his re-lationships grew cold, prospects were rained upon. And still his guard was down. Stefan, the man who was prepared for everything, who took every opportunity, who risked and ran, and fell on his feet. This man, in all innocence, had no idea, no inkling or vaguest suspicion that under the surface the iceberg menaced.

Stefan merited what awaited him, the unexpected and unwished-for future that Louise had planned for him. 'You've got it coming to you.' She would take from him the things he most coveted in life and in others: admiration, praise, acknowledgement, position, reputation. Louise would return to Stefan what he had given to her: indifference, disregard, neglect.

⋄►═◉ ◉═◄⋄

So, the circle closed. Stefan's phone rang with less frequency. Occasionally Louise would call, and still his games would continue. She wondered when he would break. 'Just a question of time,' she thought. 'Just a question of time.'

⋄►═◉ ◉═◄⋄

Now there were changes in Stefan's life. On his kitchen table, torn into tiny pieces, a letter from his publisher, telling of a book that would not be reprinted. Stefan's secret. 'It's not important,' he said as he poured his coffee. 'No, really it's not.' He would never divulge his distress, never admit a failure, not even to him-self. Especially not to Louise. Louise remembered the pride and the certainty with which Stefan had described his future post.

'Should I apply?' he had asked her, for effect, confident of her answer. Her admiration *had* counted for something in his life. Like the wife she might have been, Louise had supported him.

'Of course you should,' she had said. Who could be better than Stefan? But now the tables were turned. A colleague from overseas: he was more deserving, she thought, a more acceptable candidate.

Stefan's application was bypassed, his part stolen. 'That can't be right,' he thought. 'It must be a mistake.' A word of consolation from the dean left perplexity and frustration unresolved. So close to an achievement, so easily lost. 'It was mine,' he thought as he watched the coffee brew. 'I know it was mine.' The post was not mentioned again.

perplexity and frustration unresolved. So close to an achievement, so easily lost.

Louise did not ask. In the silence of her study, she slid a silver blade through the top of an emblazoned envelope. The letter within, on headed notepaper, was handwritten, a personal acknowledgement of a matter of some importance brought to the attention of her old professor. 'Dear Louise,' he began. 'You were right to let me know,' he wrote. 'Feel no guilt,' he continued. 'Integrity is the word,' he said. 'Action will be taken,' he assured her. She returned the letter to its envelope and set it down in orderly fashion, with others of its kind.

Louise sat at her desk and relished the fruits of her labour. 'Mmm,' she thought, 'this feels good,' and she hummed a little tune. Hers was the satisfaction of revenge, the prize of retribution. Soon, she knew, Stefan would return to her and be humbled. She knew this with confidence, and she would claim what was rightfully hers – her power to dominate, to direct, and to command respect.

'From now on,' she thought, 'you'll do as I please,' And in the setting of his sun and with the darkening of his lights, Louise rose, a radiant light, acclaimed, admired, triumphant.

'It was you all the time, holding me back,' she said as she cleared away her breakfast things. 'How foolish I was not to have seen it.'

Angry, squabbling voices resounded through the home that was once his haven and his refuge. Stefan did not fit the bill or make the grade, no longer met the expectations of a demanding partner. Stefan disappointed.

He had promised so much – except to Louise. To her, he had promised nothing and given less. She had expected a great deal once, but no more. She was far wiser now. Knowing him, Louise had learnt to live with disillusionment. We often do it ourselves. When we expect the worst, the good things come to us as pleasant gifts. That had been Louise's philosophy. Had been.

Jennifer had expected much and had received little. Stefan returned one cold Tuesday evening from the airport and found the house empty, her belongings gone.

⊷⊷◉ ◉⊷⊷

In the confusion of his newly vacant hours, the phone would ring and Stefan would hear the same voice, comforting in its familiarity and persistence.

'How are things?' she'd say.

But still he held up the mask of self-deception, maintaining a protective arrogance.

'Couldn't be better,' he'd say.

'Liar,' she'd think. 'As always.'

⊷⊷◉ ◉⊷⊷

In time Stefan would learn that it was not *he* who might take *Louise* back but, rather, *she* who took *him*. It was Louise who would deign to restore him and give support. But for now she was distant, unattainable. She was there within his reach and yet inaccessible, often on the lips of other men. Stefan could not claim she was his. Well, of course, she was not.

Louise was no-one's. She was quite unique. 'I'm special,' she would think. And her uniqueness was acknowledged within the world they shared but, above all, privately by him. And yet intimacy was denied him. What Stefan had shared and possessed before was withheld from him now. And he yearned for it.

'You are mine, Louise,' he'd think. For with all else that was once of value in his life now removed, there was nothing else: 'You were ...' And that on which he focused became the one sole desire of his heart, and Louise was the one thing he desired. For having her, all else would be restored, and the world would re-assemble and return to normality, security, and the complacency of our daily and insignificant achievements. How foolish, Stefan, to recognise now what you had before but lost.

⤙⟶◉ ◉⟵⤚

Louise replayed Stefan's voice, hollow and distant, on her answering machine.

'Call me,' he would say. 'Call me.'

But she wouldn't. 'Stew a while,' she thought. 'It'll do you good.'

⤙⟶◉ ◉⟵⤚

Stefan would hear of her. Accounts, reports, passing remarks from colleagues. Occasionally, a card from a far land – 'Dear Stefan –' - and he would scrutinise her message, read and re-read for some hidden meaning, the faintest hint of desire or tenderness – 'Love, Louise.' His memory surely did not lie. There had been a time of pursuit and longing when he could rely on her calls and invitations, when he knew Louise had been his to cast away. How had the change occurred? Could she be regained? What did she wish for now that he had not already given her? Could she continue to deny him when before she had been so voracious and violent in her passion? These and other questions raged through his mind. Yes, they did 'rage.' If you interrogate yourself too long and intensively as Stefan did, your brain begins to ache. It's hardly a pleasant feeling.

Stefan was the product of his own selfishness. He was the man who had had everything from Louise, but had neglected to hold it. Careless, Stefan. Louise knew him well now, as well as if she'd climbed inside his head and viewed the world through his eyes using the logic of his own brain.

'Where there was one woman like me, there were others. That's the way he saw it,' thought Louise. True. Stefan had seen her not as an individual but as one of many. Her passion was disposable like a paper plate. It was replaced when he had eaten.

⤙⟶◉ ◉⟵⤚

All this was true, but not in Stefan's reality. In his solitude, he re-created times past, a desire of false memories, forgetting that times past were not as this, building a past that existed only newly in his mind, a perversion of memory – a memory that Louise would have wished for, but which future ordained she should never enjoy. Memories such as these gave comfort in loneliness, and Louise collected Stefan in his loneliness, as he had once found and imprisoned her.

Like a man blind in one eye, he feared he might lose the sight of the other. Belief had failed him. Books gathered dust on his shelves, papers stacked and moved from one place to another, but still untouched. Stefan once had a certainty in all things. The enchanted time had finished now, the cycle concluded, the time allowed expired, run its course. All this with completion incomplete. Stefan looked to Louise for re-enchantment. She breathed confidence, security and warmth. He could not abide her absences, her trips away, her associations. He loathed the men who might know her and the men she might know. Louise's life beyond him was unacceptable and abhorrent. A victim of his own imagination, Stefan condemned himself to seethe and suffer like other men who desired influence but had none.

In his dreams, Stefan followed her, running faster and faster, his arm and hand and fingers stretched out before him, touching her hair, almost agonisingly arriving, but too slow to hold and keep. Louise was evasive, eluding him, deluding him, and Stefan felt his heart would burst with the excitement of the chase and the anguish of perpetual loss. And then they would come upon a huge towering wall, looming airily towards the heavens, and his body would fall upon hers and crush her violently against the coarse brick surface, grazing and ravaging her, and she would turn beneath him and press her bare skin against his, holding him there as she absorbed him into a deep trance of warmth and moisture and he, resisting and letting go rhythmically until, in that very moment that he gave himself up, she was gone. And he would see himself naked on the floor of a white tiled bathroom, his hands and face adhering to the wet clammy surface. He would raise his head and feel the cold still, an icicle on his cheek and through a haze he would see another man in his place with her, a man he recognised but did not know at all, entwining and devouring, and Stefan would scream and wrench his nails down the shiny surface of the tiles, plunging down into a damp, soft soil that enveloped his body, down, ripping into the dank sheets of his empty bed and waking in terror to the bleak light of early morning.

Men do have such strange dreams.

⊷▬◉ ◉▬◷

Louise played the game, luring him closer, reassuring, encouraging. Then a flash of anger, a rebuke: 'You're a loser, Stefan.' A hurtful acknowledgement of failing – 'Let's face it. You're a loser. That's why she left you' – but worse, of not succeeding or trying or fulfilling – 'You know it's true,' she would say. 'Why not admit it?' Louise, a wicked angel holding up the looking glass. She did want Stefan and she would have him, but she would wait and so must he.

⊷▬◉ ◉▬◷

Louise did return to Stefan, but sparingly. He, the guest in her home, not she in his. Her fervour was as before, but limited, controlled and controlling. Lying by her side, his fingertips tracing the gentle curve of her body, Stefan wished for her part in the conspiracy, else she might betray him. He heard her whispers. He closed his eyes and held her words tightly in his mind. Louise's sweetness had a bitter core, he thought, but hoped he was wrong. Their lovemaking consumed him, hiding an unfamiliar depth and bringing him melancholy.

The pain! But surely men such as Stefan do not feel pain ... cannot feel pain ... are not supposed to? But who can say if men truly have such emotions as these or if these emotions are sincere or merely endured for their own tormented enjoyment.

Stefan was in a dark pool, his feet waving and pushing through the water towards the bottom, but never touching, stretching for something he knew was there but could never quite reach and continuing his effort even as the water sealed its waves shut over his head. Slashes of light from above dwindled into dim slits of hope and his eyes would close and his heart would cease to beat in that silent blackness. Tough, Stefan. It's tough.

A man cannot truly love if he has the body but not the mind. Louise's was the profoundest of punishments.

Stefan searched for joy, but found sorrow with no discernible cause. Louise was remote. Could she doubt his commitment? Stefan doubted hers. There were boundaries, fences, borders. He dared not cross or assail them. If you were a prisoner, would you risk your privileges? And, just as Stefan searched for meaning in Louise's words, he now sought sentiment in the everyday things that surrounded her.

'Do I equal their importance?' he asked himself. He was pitiful. Ideas mattered now that had never occurred to him before, that he might be a living being like a possession, an object of desire, but not more. 'Surely not,' he told himself.

So, what of Louise's feelings? Did *they* translate into thoughts and the thoughts into words unspoken to him, written perhaps, and what did *they* reveal that he could not know through touching her, holding her, being with her and within her, penetrating and yet not penetrating the deep channel to her soul? Louise's soul. What folly to expect a soul as well as a body, and yet some men do!

Stefan turned the pages of an address book. He knew he should not. 'Don't do that,' he told himself – this was his good voice. Another nagged on. How many acquaintances? How many lovers? Stefan slammed the book shut. Letters offered greater hazards. Louise had stacked them neatly, personal letters, he supposed. New letters near, old letters far. Foreign stamps and postmarks. Long, typed envelopes and small handwritten ones, thin folded sheets, whites and blues and creams, rich glossy papers, dense heavy leaves bearing embossed addresses. Stefan looked, but did not touch. He stared. He wondered if he dared ... to reach out, select, read and know. 'It's wrong.' he thought. He knew it was wrong. He took no decision. His hand moved mechanically, searching and inspecting. He drank in information, greetings, invitations, reflections, inquiries.

There was nothing of significance, nothing to fan his jealousy. 'There you are. Told you.' Stefan thought himself cheated.

And then he came to one familiar but unexpected envelope.

'What's this?' he thought and paused, his breath quickening and his brain and heart first in argument, then in fierce combat.

The letter was before him, a personal letter, addressing Louise by name. 'My dear Louise,' it began. Stefan swept the page, skimming swiftly from left to right, his eyes taking in everything and nothing, up and down, looking, focusing, interpreting and understanding the tight inscrutable writing of deception and betrayal, a secret knowledge passed between two people resolving, irrevocably, the destiny of a third. Destruction through words and promises. 'Action will be taken,' the letter assured him.

How would you have felt? And if you had been *Stefan*, how would you have felt? Stefan's world trembled. Who would begrudge Stefan his moment of drama now? And this trembling – let us call it that – this trembling was a dull ponderous thud from the heavy outer door, vibrating upwards to where he sat immobile in Louise's chair. Was she to find him there with the letter in his hand? Her footsteps echoed distantly. Then, approaching, they grew louder, and louder also the noise in Stefan's head as the palm of his hand slid slowly across the leather table top and his fingertips touched the smooth, steel blade of the letter opener. And then he listened to hear Louise's key in the lock, searching and scratching, finding its way, about to enter there where she knew he would be waiting.

'I'm here, waiting for you.'

Stefan was waiting for Louise, you see. For the writing of wrongs.

⊷▬◉ ◉▬⊶

Magpies

THE FOUR OF us were on our way up to the penthouse suite when the lift juddered to a halt somewhere between the seventh and eighth floors. We were already late after we had foolishly congregated in the ladies' restroom along the corridor from the Delfont Lounge, where the cravat man had been initiating us into the joys of tie making, the history, the fabric, and the manner of tying ties. We had been lured to the presentation by the promise of a free lunch and a designer tie. What folly! Surely we had better things to do.

I was there only because I was covering the event for one of the Sunday supplements. Still, I could easily have left after the presentation and not ended up stuck in the lift with the other three, but greed had brought me thus far.

The accountant, who had so carefully redrawn her taut lips in the bathroom mirror, now pursed them nervously … for who was to say when we would be released? It was fortuitous that we had had the good sense to make use of the facilities before ascending to the limbo of the seventh and eighth.

'I should never have come,' said the web designer, sylph-like and blonde, 'but since it was only down the road from the office, I thought I would risk slipping out for a couple of hours.'

I leaned on the emergency button until we heard a great deal of activity above us, shouts of reassurance and promises of an early release.

'An early release and lunch too, I hope,' said the accountant.

'Yes, I'm starved,' said the web designer. 'I didn't have breakfast.' To look at her, you'd say she didn't ever have breakfast, and probably not lunch or dinner either.

The fourth woman said nothing. She gave a sigh and removed a packet of cigarettes from her bag.

'You can't smoke those in here,' said web girl.

'Who says?' said the woman, placing the cigarette between her lips.

'Oxygen may be limited,' said the accountant. 'We could suffocate.'

'Do me a favour!' said the woman. 'All I want are a few quick puffs.'

'No,' I said, 'you'll set off the fire alarms, and then we'll not only be stuck, but rained on too.'

'And I've just had my colour done,' said the accountant.

The woman threw the cigarette back in her bag and leaned against the wall of the lift. 'All right,' she said, 'and what do we do now? Sing hymns, recite poetry? Bond?'

'We could sit down, get comfortable and phone home,' I said. I thought that was quite clever of me. If someone had started to scream I could have slapped their face and said, "Pull yourself together, woman," but no such luck.

'No signal,' said the accountant from her oak-panelled corner of the lift floor.

'I don't even like ties,' said web girl, studying her reflection in the bottom of the wall-length mirror and adjusting her blonde fringe. 'Very difficult to fiddle with!' She turned to look at me. 'My name's Selene by the way.'

'I'm Phoebe,' I said. 'And ties are useful as Christmas presents for the men in our lives.'

'I'm Helena,' said the accountant. 'I can't just buy *any* tie. My husband can spot an Armani from a Debenhams at a hundred yards. Other people learn about the knots in carpets and I learn about the knots in ties. How sad is that?'

We turned to look at the fourth woman.

'Why are you looking at me?' she said.

'You haven't told us your name or why you're here,' I said.

'Yes, who are you buying for?' said Selene.

'My name's Diana,' said the woman, 'and I come not to buy for men, but to meet them.'

So there we were: Helena the accountant, Selene the web girl, me … journalist extraordinaire, and Diana, all of us seated on the lift floor as if awaiting the arrival of the grand pasha.

'And what did you say you do, Diana?' I said.

'I didn't,' said Diana.

'A woman of few words,' I said.

Diana smiled. No, actually, she didn't. She smirked.

We were in for the long haul. From time to time the lift shuddered. We trusted it would not hurtle without warning into the basement, and that it was just a question of time before we emerged like the rescued crew of a disabled submarine. We fell silent. Helena cleared her throat, propped her head against the wall and stared at the ceiling. Selene sniffed a little and looked about her. I leaned on one elbow and drummed the fingers of my other hand on the floor.

'One would assume,' said Diana, 'that a tie promotion of this import would attract more men, but as luck would have it, I ended up imprisoned in this lift with three women.'

'Well, pardon us for our gender,' said Helena.

'Very disappointing for you,' said Selene.

Diana fixed Selene for a moment, her expression one of puzzlement and disdain.

'What?' said Selene, staring back.

I spoke up in an attempt to break the ice. 'Had there been men here,' I said, 'I'm sure the conversation would have been most congenial.'

'Since it isn't,' began Diana, but then she paused. She was again studying Selene, as if chewing something over. Selene for her part had turned her attention to the contents of her bag, rummaging inside, looking for heaven knows what.

'Since it isn't, what?' I said.

Diana turned to look at me. 'Since we shall obviously be here for some time, I feel inclined to take pity on you, and tell you all a story.'

'A story about …?' I said.

'About the friendship of women and the love of men. Or, in this case, the love of one man in particular.'

'Carry on. Carry on,' said Helena. 'If we must wait an eternity for release, we may as well be entertained. This will be entertaining, won't it?'

As the hammering and clamouring continued somewhere above us, we made ourselves comfortable and Diana began her story.

'I'm going to tell you about the evening I visited my friend Judy. In a sense, the events of that evening were what brought me here today. There is a connection between then and now as you'll see. Judy and I had once been very close. We were at school together and we had shared the joys and disappointments of early flirtations. We went our separate ways, but from time to time we bumped into each other and exchanged confidences. The course of true love always seemed to flow more smoothly for her than for me. I felt slightly envious of her good fortune, specifically the stability of her relationships. But over the years I came to appreciate that she felt slightly envious of me, specifically of the multiplicity of my relationships. You might well ask yourselves if it is better to have one enduring partnership or many tumultuous affairs. Are you inclined to opt for sameness or variety?'

'Well,' began Selene.

'I think that's meant to be a rhetorical question, Selene,' I said.

'It is,' said Diana. 'Let me cut to the chase. Or rather, to that evening's visit.'

'I wasn't there by chance. The lights of the flat were on. They – Judy and her partner – were the kind of people who stayed minimal and curtainless. From across the street you could see into their flat. I know. I'd seen into it myself. Many times. I knew Judy was in that evening, just as I knew he was out. She opened the door to me herself. They didn't have a door phone. Heaven knows why. They had plenty of money.

'"Well! Hello, stranger," she said with evident delight. "What brings you here? Haven't seen you in yonks." I think she was both surprised and pleased to see me there on her doorstep fresh from the sales with my large carrier bag. I apologised for my long absence from her life. It had been months, maybe even a year or more.

'"I've just been so tied up," I told her. "You know how it is."

'She ushered me in through the door and then along a little passage, chattering all the way, past a lady's bicycle, a pair of wellies – hers presumably, not his – a crate of miscellaneous wine bottles, all empty. They evidently consumed a lot, what with the dinner parties, which you could see from across the street, and the unexpected visitors. Maybe I overdid the explanations a little but I doubt that she noticed.

'"I was supposed to meet a friend," I told her, "but they cancelled and then of course it dawned on me that I was in your part of town and so I thought to myself, well, why not pop round and say hello to Judy?"'

'I can't say I'm too fond of people turning up on my doorstep unexpectedly,' Helena interrupted. Already she was looking a little more relaxed. She'd unbuttoned her jacket, folded it and placed it carefully beside her on the floor. 'You usually have to feed surprise visitors, or at least offer to feed them and hope they'll decline.'

'Yes, well, I wasn't there for a free dinner,' said Diana.

'Go on,' I said.

'Judy guided me along the narrow corridor past the Barbours hanging in the hallway, and then she led the way at a run up the thickly carpeted stairs into her expansive and very impressive lounge. Perhaps she expected me to comment, or to compliment her on her flat – *their* flat – but I didn't. I dropped my bags on the floor and slipped into the corner of one of their white leather sofas. I felt very comfortable. Just as if I'd been in the familiar surroundings of my own home.'

'Ah! Such self-assurance,' said Helena. 'That always flaws people. The more confident and sophisticated you are, the more awkward the other party feels.'

'Not always,' said Selene.

'Let's just listen to Diana's story, shall we?' I said. I had a sense that Diana might turn strange – stranger than she was already – if someone annoyed her enough.

Diana raised her eyebrows and continued. 'Judy told me I looked great. I *did* look great, which is more than I could say for her. She was pretty. No doubt about that. But she was starting to look a trifle haggard.'

'Oh, I know,' said Helena. 'The way you do when you're running around after one man all the time.' Selene gave a snigger, and I a knowing nod.

'"What's your secret?" she asked me. "Must be love!" she said, and she giggled. And then it was just like old times – the two of us together again, opening a bottle of wine, remembering all those past jobs and journeys and boyfriends and lovers.

'I told her I thought the flat was looking lovely. She liked that. I got up to have a look at the pictures on the walls. I ran my fingers along the spines of all those worthy books on their sparkly chrome and glass shelves.

'"There's still lots to do," said Judy, "but I just never seem to have the time." I didn't suppose this was all her work. Did she choose the watercolours? No. I know for a fact she didn't. On the sideboard there was a photo in a mahogany frame of the two of them together.

'"So," I said, "you're still with Gerard, then?"

'She gave a sigh. I could only describe it as a sigh of resignation. "Yes," she said. "Still with Gerard. What about you?"

'I remember taking a cigarette from the little carved wooden box on Judy's bureau. It was next to her sewing things. I never did take Judy for a seamstress. What, did she sit there on cold London evenings embroidering hearts and cherries on armchair covers? I couldn't see it myself. I slid back into my place on the sofa. "What about me?" I said. "Oh, nothing special. You'll remember Peter, of course. I soon ditched him. Quite a bit out of pocket too, and I had to move all my things out of that ghastly house of his in Shepherd's Bush."

'I never liked Shepherd's Bush,' said Helena.

'It's very up-market these days,' I said.

'That may well be,' said Helena, 'but I still wouldn't want to live there.'

'Neither would I,' said Diana, 'and anyway Peter didn't have a job so he couldn't do it up. It was bye-bye, Peter, and hello, Nick. Except that Nick and I never *did* see eye-to-eye, so that didn't last very long. A pity, because he'd just bought a rather grand house in Chiswick.'

'By the river?' I said. 'What a shame.'

'Yes,' said Diana. 'That's exactly what Judy said. She was always good at commiserating. Then she said to me, "So, now there's no one then." I believe she was genuinely concerned. "There *was* no one," I told her, "until..."

'"Until?"

'"Until the *new* man came along," I told her.'

'Well, the new man is only new until you find out he's much the same as all the others,' said Helena.

'Cynicism never got anyone anywhere,' I said.

'You'll find that it does,' said Helena, 'and it provides a great deal of psychological relief.'

Before Diana could open her mouth to comment, voices were heard from on high.

'Oh, heavenly voices,' said Helena. 'We are saved!'

'Ladies,' said the voice, 'this is the assistant manager speaking. Can you hear me?'

'Yes, we hear you,' I said.

'We're terribly sorry about all this. We'll have you out in no time,' he said. 'Is there anything I can get you?'

'Yes, send down a couple of bottles of champagne,' shouted Helena.

'I can't drink any champagne,' said Selene. 'It'll make me want to go to the loo.'

'Don't worry,' said Helena. 'I'll drink yours, darling.'

Diana gave a sigh. 'Do you want me to finish this story or not?' she said.

'I want to hear the story,' I said. 'I want to hear about this new man.'

'The new man reference went down really well with Judy,' said Diana. 'She tucked her feet under her on the sofa – as I knew she would – and she lifted the wine glass to her lips. I refilled my own, and reflected. Judy was just sitting there all agog.'

'"Well," she said, "tell me!"

'"There's not a lot to tell," I said. "Not really." I stood up and wandered to the window. I had decided to draw this out as long as possible. "It happened about a year ago," I told her. "We were introduced by a … a friend. Some 'do' we were at – at some gallery or other – Knightsbridge I think."

'I took my time. I remember gazing out for a moment at the health bar on the other side of the road, and at the row of neighbouring antique shops glistening in the fading light of day. I turned my back on the window and stubbed out my cigarette in the tiny silver ashtray on the dining table.'

'Where did she live, this Judy?' said Selene.

'North London, I would imagine,' said Helena.

'West London,' said Diana.

'That's what *I* thought,' said Selene. 'I know that area quite well.'

'Well, whatever!' said Diana. 'This is about the man, not the place. I told Judy, "The moment I saw him I thought, 'That's him. He's the one.' There was something about him, something that appealed to me, but that, you know, that wouldn't necessarily be everyone's cup of tea."

"'Oh, right! X-factor," said Judy. She knew exactly.

"'X-factor. Yes, that's it," I said. "He had a sort of arrogance about him. I knew he was interested. Right from that first meeting he was weighing me up and down. He was obviously quite certain that I'd fall for him. And he was right. We had lunch together that day and then afternoon tea, and then an evening drink. The time just flew. He offered to drive me home. I... accepted." I paused at this point.'

"'And?" said Judy.

"'Nothing," I said. "It all seemed so perfect and neither of us wanted to, you know, rush things."

'Judy seemed a little disappointed. She shifted slightly in her seat and took another sip of wine. I moved back towards the sofa. I put down my glass, delved for a moment in my bag and took out an ornate silver cigarette case. I flipped open the lid and removed a cigarette.

"'He gave me this," I said, handing the case to Judy. "This and lots of other things. Expensive gifts, many of them. Perfume too. Here," I said, and I leaned across the coffee table and held out my wrist for Judy to sniff.

"'Boucheron," she said. "My favourite."

'I slumped back into the sofa, lit my cigarette and billowed out a haze of smoke.'

'That's a bit cheeky,' said Helena.

'The smoking?' said Diana.

'I can't abide people smoking in my house,' said Helena.

'He must have smoked,' I said. 'Gerard, I mean. Ashtrays all over the place.'

'I used to smoke,' said Selene. 'Gave it up.'

'Better for your skin,' said Helena.

'Right,' said Selene.

'Have you quite finished?' said Diana.

'Sorry,' I said.

Diana lifted a small bottle of water from her bag, unscrewed the top and took a swig. 'I told Judy about the phone calls. The man would call me almost every day at the office. "Your new man's on the phone," they'd say to me. It became a bit of a joke. But, you know, I was beginning to get a taste for it. I looked forward to those calls. I told Judy about the dinners we had together, how the man was quite fond of obscure little bistros with designer food. I remember tapping the ash of my cigarette into Judy's onyx ashtray, and I remember that I picked up an auction catalogue from the coffee table and thumbed through it. And all the while, Judy was there sipping her wine, fixed on me, her eyes wide and hopeful as a child's.

'"And then it began," I told her. "Your classic wild affair. Of course," I said, "I'd guessed he was married or, at least, tied in some way. Our times together were so limited. It didn't take long to work that out."

'"Oh, Diana," wailed Judy. "Poor you! What did you do?"

'"I asked him," I said.

'"Oh, God!" Judy said.

'Perhaps she couldn't believe I'd be so bold.

'"Yes, all right," he said. "It's true. I live with someone. We'd been going out for years and then in the end we moved in together."

'"What a shit!" said Judy.'

'What a shit!' said Selene.

'Oh, doesn't surprise me in the least,' said Helena.

'I hope you took the cue and left it alone when you found out he was with someone.' I said.

'There seemed to be no indication that either of them would be moving out, but I was hooked by then, you see.' Diana hesitated for a moment. 'I suppose you could say I was infatuated. I told Judy.

'"And?" she said.

'I told her how the affair had carried on. I texted him. He texted me. He called me. I called him. But always at the office. I didn't want to rock the boat by calling him at home. I didn't want him to think he couldn't trust me.

'"You didn't want him to think he couldn't trust you to keep a secret," Judy said.

'"I wanted more of him," I told her, "but he didn't seem to want more of me." I felt quite choked when I told her that. She must have picked that up in my voice.

'"Well, he wouldn't, would he?" Judy said. "He had two of you." She was curled up on the sofa frowning into her wine glass. "What a bastard," she said.

'Yes, what a bastard,' said Selene.

'I still think you should have ended it with him there and then,' said Helena.

'I told you how I felt. I was infatuated with him. He was even leaving his things at my house, his shirts, his socks … his ties.'

'This story's getting worse,' I said.

'In the end, I did call him at home,' said Diana.

'Goodness,' said Helena.

'Judy was equally shocked when I told her. "Oh, Diana!" she said.

'"I very nearly blew his cover," I told her. I was out of my mind with... with...'

'With frustration?' said Helena.

'Frustration. Yes. He said it was okay, but I knew I'd scared him. A week later I got an e-mail. "It's been wonderful," he said, "but let's leave it at that. Let's keep it as a great friendship."'

'Oh, please,' said Selene in disgust.

'I just blew a fuse,' said Diana.

'I should think so,' I said.

'I told Judy how we'd had a showdown after that. "You can't play around with people's emotions like that," I told him. "Do you think you can just go picking people up and dumping them back down again? Who the Hell do you think you are?" I said. I didn't let him off the hook. Not at all. Half an hour of that and he was back where I wanted him – all love and kisses and "I didn't mean what I said. I've been under a lot of stress," and all that rubbish.

'But months passed and things changed. All the time I was telling her this, Judy's face was crinkled with indignation. I told her how I'd had the growing sense that he was, I don't know, playing along with me. That he was hiding something. He'd tell me lies. I didn't cotton on at first. He was good at hiding things. He'd had a lot of practice. He was meeting other women, you see.'

'God,' said Selene, half in surprise, half in disgust.

'Well, that figures,' said Helena.

'Judy was dismayed. "Oh, Diana," she said to me. "More than one?"

'"Yes," I told her.

"I see."

'"Do you?" I said.

'And then she said, "It's awful. I don't know what I'd do. If it was me, I mean."

There was a loud clatter from above. As one, we tilted our heads and looked at the ceiling. A square of panelling was dislodging itself. Behind it we saw an area of darkness and then an amorphous shape wriggling in the gloom. The object came closer and then it was buffeted against the sides of the opening. A large wicker basket descended, down and down until it landed with a bump at our feet. Inside were two bottles of champagne, a set of elegant crystal glasses and a selection of antipasti packed in ice.

'*Deus ex machine*,' proclaimed Helena.

'No,' said Selene cautiously. 'It's Veuve Cliquot.'

'Never mind. Just open the bottle, dear,' said Helena.

'All right, ladies?' shouted a voice. 'Not long now. We'll soon have you out of there!'

Few sensations are more pleasurable than that of ice cold champagne trickling down a parched throat. For the next ten minutes or so we appeased our senses and lost the plot.

'So, what happened next?' I said, as I spooned caviar onto a tiny cracker.

'One thing I wanted to know,' said Selene. 'Are these their real names? I mean is Judy Judy and is Gerard Gerard?'

Diana stared at her. Selene wrinkled her brow.

'No,' said Diana, 'the names have been changed to protect the guilty.'

'Oh,' said Selene.

'Let's re-cap,' said Helena. 'You're there in Judy's lounge, and you're telling her that this new man, whose name is …. What *is* his name?'

'I didn't say,' said Diana.

'All right. You're telling Judy that this new man had been giving you the run-around, that he had been seeing other women, not just you.'

'Yes,' said Diana.

'And Judy thought that was awful,' I said.

'We all think it's awful,' said Helena, 'but as women of the world, we're not that surprised.'

'They're easily found out.' I said. 'There are usually clues of various sorts.'

'There were,' said Diana. 'I told Judy how I'd gone to a pub not far from her house to meet some colleagues, and I'd seen him. He was there chatting up some simpering blonde, leaning over her, lighting her cigarette. And she was just one of the many. He'd been messing about all the time. I just hadn't twigged it. Judy was transfixed.'

Diana gave a sigh at this point and closed her eyes.

'Blind. That's what I was. I told Judy how I had gone straight home and collected up the letters and the presents – all the things he'd given me. I threw them into a carrier bag and I drove round to his flat. The lights were on. His girlfriend was in. I rang the bell.

'Then, sitting there on Judy's sofa, I reached down to the green bag I'd brought with me. Judy's face darkened. She sat bolt upright.

'"And here I am," I said to her. "And here you are, and here's the carrier bag and the letters and the gifts. And Gerard? Well, he's down at the Archer's Tavern with that blonde. Maybe you'll want to go down there and take a look."'

'Oh my God!' said Helena, nearly choking on her smoked salmon.

I burst out laughing.

Selene was silent. She had gone quite pale. She looked at Diana without saying a word and then her eyes became transparent and watery. Two large tears rolled down her cheeks.

'You bitch,' she hissed. 'You bitch. It was you. You sent her—'

Diana opened her lips to reply, but then the lift lurched suddenly upwards. An empty champagne bottle rolled across the lift floor. A glass flipped over and smashed, spilling its fizzling contents around our feet. We grasped for the walls but there was nothing to hold and we were propelled against each other. And then, as suddenly as the movement had started, it stopped. A few seconds passed in which we smoothed our ruffled hair and straightened our crumpled clothing. The lift doors sprang open and we emerged to the sound of unrestrained applause.

In the ensuing confusion we were engulfed by our fellow tie collectors, and their tide of enthusiasm carried us down the corridor to our promised lunch. Selene was lost in the bustle. No one saw her go.

Helena hugged me goodbye before she climbed into her Lexus, the rear seat packed with complimentary gift-wrapped ties and a gigantic food hamper. Diana and I watched her drive away.

'Well, keep in touch,' I said to Diana as we stood in the foyer of the store.

'You too,' said Diana. She gave me a peck-like kiss on the cheek and turned to go.

'You never told us—'

'What I do?' said Diana. 'Let's say I'm a collector.'

'A collector?'

'I collect ties.'

'With the men still in them.'

She laughed and walked away in the direction of Menswear.

⊰══⊱ ⊰══⊱

The Moon Cat

She was never that keen on the cat – not at first. It was spooky. It had sparkly green eyes that glowed in the dark, and when you switched on the light, it wasn't there. It was somewhere else where you hadn't expected it to be – on top of a wardrobe or under an armchair.

'I don't know why you keep it if it gives you the creeps,' said Eliot, his head tipped upside down between his feet like a contortionist, trying to see where the animal had gone.

When Charlotte was at work, Eliot would growl at the cat and chase it from the room. Charlotte felt obliged to keep it. She was superstitious. Lying in bed the night after her mother's funeral, she'd seen him at her window on the fifth floor, staring in at her with those fluorescent emerald eyes, the tufts of his coat glistening with the warm moon rays that flooded into her room and bathed her carpet. She somehow thought he had been sent to look after her.

He's here just for me, she thought. Though it looked to be the other way around.

She fed him. She talked to him. He listened and he looked, but he never came close enough to be stroked. She would have liked to touch him though the hairs stood up on the back of her neck as soon as she moved close. He looked unpredictable as only a stray animal can.

'He's wild,' said Eliot. 'You should get rid of him. He'd scratch a baby's eyes out.'

'We don't have a baby,' said Charlotte.

'Well, any baby,' said Eliot. 'He's vicious.'

The cat hissed and slunk from the room.

Eliot had no cause to criticise. He spent his days watching TV. When he went to the kitchen, the cat watched him as he ate and Eliot teased him by dangling pieces of ham in front of his nose and then snatching them away. Perhaps he would have done worse, but he could never catch the beast. It would vanish without trace. Eliot would resume his place in front of the television and look about uncomfortably.

When Charlotte left in the morning she would lock the door of the flat behind her. When she returned, the cat would be waiting for her on the stairs.

'Did you let the cat out?' she'd say to Eliot.

'Nope,' he'd say and switch channels, and turn up the volume.

Once she came in the door and gave herself a fright. The shock must have showed on her face.

'What's the matter with you?' said Eliot.

'Nothing,' she said, but she could have told him that she'd seen her mother there, sitting at the kitchen table in her dressing gown, waiting, and staring across the room at Eliot. She looked again. It wasn't her mother. Her heart beat loudly and heavily. No, it wasn't her mother – it was the cat.

'I'm sick of that cat trailing its bloody tail in my cornflakes,' said Eliot. 'I don't want to see him anymore,' he said.

She did nothing. She couldn't bear to part with the cat now. She'd grown used to him. She wasn't so sure about Eliot though.

That night, as Eliot lay in a drunken stupor across her bed, she stood in her kitchen and gazed across the roof tops and at the wide white moon and the silhouetted chimneys and aerials and satellite dishes, and she fancied she saw a cat like hers on a distant roof top and she knew without the slightest doubt that it *was* her cat and that he *was* pure magic. For now she realised that when she saw him, she didn't see him. And, when she didn't see him he was there, and when he was up, he was down ... and when he was down, he was up ... and he was in two rooms at the same time or not there at all. And he was in the street following her ... and in her office, sitting at her feet ... and in the tube and on the bus. And she felt a strange tranquillity. And that night, as on the many nights she had forgotten, she felt his paws treading softly across her body, and she heard his voiceless purr in her ear, and her breathing became his breathing.

And when she awoke, she knew she was alone, but she was glad of it. She felt Eliot's body lifeless beside hers and she saw the soft curled body of the cat sleeping peacefully across Eliot's face, breathing the breath that Eliot no longer breathed, and then she did not see him. But she knew he was there and not there. Just for her.

Mirror Image

'WE WON'T BE seeing much of each other over the next few weeks.'

He gave her the news casually, then reached for his lighter and lit his next cigarette.

'No?' she replied.

'I'm going away for a few days,' he said, and then paused. 'I'll be back for Christmas.' He inhaled, leaned his head back, closed his eyes, and blew the smoke up into the air. It twirled up against the embossed surface of the plum-coloured walls.

Barbara watched it rise and waited.

Without opening his eyes, he said, 'I'm bringing my mother back. Just for a few weeks.'

'Oh,' she replied, and she smiled — as a formality, though she knew he did not see her smile. She could think of nothing else to say. Excluded, she was a tiny part of a secret life of his. She was not... Not close. However close she felt she had been, however much of her intimacy she had given to him, she knew he did not regard her as close. She was not family, or intended as family. She was not intended for the kind of closeness she herself desired.

That evening was short and bitter in her memory. As he often did, he glanced at his watch, rose to his feet, and with the cigarette still between his lips, he gathered up his belongings — his keys, his cigarettes, his lighter — thrusting them quickly into his overcoat pocket.

'I have to go,' he said.

What she wanted was to have some hold over him, to freeze him in time and re-live his presence. She would have him bound to her permanently, returning always on an invisible link of desire and commitment. He had no such ties and was bound by no one. He made sure of that. Family was his only commitment. It was his duty. He was duty bound.

Barbara imagined him on the plane as he travelled home – shuffling his papers, making notes and considering the enjoyment to come. Perhaps he thought of her, but, most probably he did not. She saw him in the local bar, drinking with his friends. They would be married, she supposed. They would envy his freedom and urge him to recount his conquests. Would he speak of her, she wondered, or would there be better stories to be told?

She visualised his flirting with other women, his way of leaning close, speaking softly, of brushing his shoulder against theirs, a certain look in his eyes. Would he share with others those same experiences she had known? She felt he would. She was a powerless victim of her own imagination.

Then she would see him coming home to mother, in all innocence – mother's sweet boy, who smiled and kissed her on the forehead and praised her for the richness and the generosity of her cooking, and the warmth of her heart. A warmth that had not been his to inherit.

⤞ ⤝

And so the holiday came. Silent icy mornings when your breath hovered in the air before you, and when good working people stayed at home, sleeping and dreaming in their comfortable beds to refuel for the coming year.

The days were vacant without him, desirous moments unfulfilled. And with her own direction undefined, Barbara led her father into the park and, without speaking, they walked side-by-side, gazing at the hard black earth and the patches of white between the branches of naked trees. For the old man, she was sure, the days were as one. Barbara sought a distinction between night and day. She had a future of sorts. His future was behind him. Together they walked to fill the spaces in the day and to return, without weight of conscience, to their memories.

Barbara imagined her lover by her side. Her thoughts were vivid. He was solid and tangible. In this isolation of the mind she could feel his breath on her face, the gentle pressure of his hand on her neck as he drew her towards him.

She was inside his world and he was enveloped within hers, a lover visible only to her, created by her heart and conjured by her brain. Other women, too, must hide secret lovers – men of private worlds past and future. And she thought of her father and his empty shell-like world, pitying him his lost imagination. She found him self-centred and indifferent. She thought him shallow and impoverished, like a man who had gambled with life and lost. She had nothing in reality, but he had even less.

And it was there in that limbo, an arid winter world of the soul, that these two met their distorted mirror image – a solitary silent man, and his mother.

As they came face-to-face, Barbara tried to sound calm and unmoved, though she was not. 'So, you're back,' she said and felt the idiocy of what she had said. In her head she was saying, 'I didn't know you were back, or that I would meet you here today, or that you would be as you are.' She had so much to say to him that would remain unvoiced.

He cut her short, showing no desire to be exposed or embarrassed by their meeting. 'Yes,' he said and he turned, unlinking his arm from that of the elderly woman by his side. 'This,' he said in haste, 'is my mother.' He looked down towards the woman, as if seeking her compliance, expecting some acknowledgement from her.

The woman stared but said nothing. Barbara followed her gaze to the old man who stood before her and heard her address him carefully and quietly.

'You said we might not meet again.'

The old man hesitated. 'I never believed we would. Never.' Then he added, 'This is my daughter.'

The elderly woman considered Barbara for a moment and smiled. There was a wisdom in the woman's eyes that Barbara could not fathom.

'And this,' said the old woman, indicating the man by her side, 'this is our son.'

⊷═◉ ◉═⊶

Class Act

Class Act I: Sarah

THE CLASS WAS full this afternoon, but much of the mystique has gone from it for me. The people are all rather dull. 'Mystique' is hardly the word.

Rebecca and Claire must have been greatly put out to see me arrive when they had probably thought I would not come at all – possibly ever – after their damning critique of my story in the last session. They can think again. I will not be bullied.

As per Michael's suggestion last week, everyone had brought crisps and peanuts, and I noted that the table was all a-clutter with budget wines. I did not touch any of them. I had taken that awful bottle of Lambrusco with me – to get rid of it, of course. I cannot quite recall how long it has been in the bottom of the kitchen cupboard.

Michael, I thought, looked just a little the worse for wear. Rebecca, as always – I regret to say – was in good form. The words 'cheeky' and 'perky' sprang to mind, but also 'sneaky' and 'scheming.'

I had been in the room only a few moments when I realised that Hussein was there too. He turned around to attract my attention. I smiled at him but not with my usual resounding enthusiasm. Yes, I will admit he is attractive, but get thee behind me. Rebecca smiled across the table at me too. She has a fair nerve.

Claire read her story and we all agreed it was excellent. Alcohol, Lambrusco or similar, helps. Rebecca positively gushed with good will – or should I say festive spirit? But then Doris had to put her foot in it by saying that she was 'unsure about the relationship between the two characters.'

'Oh, but I felt it was so absolutely clear,' said Rebecca. 'It couldn't be more clear. You can feel the depth, the intimacy.' She gushed so much that that I do declare she flowed right over the top. 'You can feel that she once had a very deep passion for this man.'

'Sorry, Rebecca,' I said – I could not let her get away with that – 'what evidence do you have of this deep passion of hers? I can't see it myself.'

She gave me the evil eye, but at least my rebuff seemed to subdue her for a while. It proved my point that, as was so often the case, she did not know what the hell she was talking about. The discussion went on at length, as it always does, and then, since it was getting late, we broke for coffee. Unusually, Rebecca remained in the room. Normally she goes down to the coffee bar. Obviously a motive there.

'Sit next to me,' said Hussein. 'I like you to be close to me.'

He gave me a sly little smile and tugged at a nearby chair. I twitched my nose in a semi-sneer and took a seat by the radiator. I acted as though distracted, but it was simply a way of avoiding direct contact. What on earth was he expecting with Rebecca sitting there? He leered back, then busied himself with his mobile phone. I consulted my diary, chewed the end of my pen, looked as clever as I could and wrote a note to the cleaning lady.

Meanwhile there was no sign of Kate, who was supposed to come and talk to us about agents. Somehow I did not think she would want to come. What could be less inviting than an end of term classroom party with a set of unpublished manic-depressive novelists asking her impossible questions and waving unfinished manuscripts in front of her nose?

Kate, look, look, my magnum opus!

I must try not to be too ungracious. She was ill apparently. When Michael explained this to us in his garbled way, Doris leaned over to me and whispered, 'She got the sack. That's why she's not coming. No point really.' Poor Kate was therefore of no further use to us.

In her absence, Michael had decided he would talk to us himself about publishers. In his state of mid-party inebriation, this was not a good idea. As he droned on, Julian was decorating a polystyrene cup with his blue Biro, Claire was drawing Alfred, and not very flatteringly at that, and Bill was looking through the contents of his briefcase. The others munched their crisps contentedly, slopped wine into paper cups leaving fine red splashes on the table, rustled cold mince pies out of their cellophane wrappers. Lindy, the plump little American woman, checked in a tiny black mirror that her lipstick had not smudged. Dave, sitting bolt upright in his chair, twitched nervously and drummed his fingers on his Lion King ring binder. The class had suspended creativity and was effectively on hold. I checked my watch from time to time and thought about the magical laws of attraction and how they seemed not to be working on this occasion.

Just before five, Bill closed his notebook and reached for his briefcase. I also closed my notebook. Nothing had been said that was worthy enough to write about. Hussein stood up and put on his coat. Rebecca draped a silk scarf around her neck and drew her fingers through her dark abundant curls, ruffling them first to the right and then to the left. I'm assuming she doesn't have a dandruff problem.

'I think we'll call it a day,' said Michael, but his words were drowned out by the screeching of hastily moved chairs. Alfred searched under Lindy's feet for his green tartan duffle bag. Doris popped Julian's pen into her handbag. Julian looked for his pen. I stood about, wondering what to do next. Michael was already hurrying down the corridor to the Gents'. There was no one here with whom I would care to walk to the pub except perhaps for Dave. I had no option but to exit with Rebecca and Hussein. Hussein caught my eye. If he was trying to tell me something, he was using the wrong language. I walked ahead of them down the stairs. I could hear Rebecca rattling on about something or other. Bless her, she has found her soulmate, I told myself. At the bottom of the stairs, I stepped through the swing doors before them. Doris was standing in the foyer putting on her coat.

'I was so worried,' she said, 'I left my coat in the cafeteria and I had my bank card and keys in the pockets.'

I feigned concern. Well, perhaps I was slightly concerned, but probably not so much about Doris as about Rebecca and Hussein. I had a sense that Rebecca would be one-up on me and the feeling was most irritating.

'Now I can't find my bus pass,' said Doris, with an anxious expression bathing her face.

As the doors swung behind me, and Rebecca and Hussein walked past, across the foyer and out of the door, I was saying to her, 'Have you looked in your cardigan pockets?' It never does to spend time flapping about around lost people. You just end up getting left behind yourself. I packed Doris back off to the cafeteria and hoped that was the last I would see of her until next term.

Dave was the next – and last – one through the doors, flustered and flushed. I knew not why.

'I do hope you are going to the pub,' I said.

He was. Any port in a storm. I did hate the idea of arriving on my own. Outside by the entrance, we found an indecisive and deflated Rebecca, and no sign at all of Hussein. I suspect she had been under the impression that she had Hussein all to herself, and then he had decided to go straight home. It seemed in character, but clearly it was not what she had expected, and her surprise had translated into disappointment. I understood then that what he did once he would do again – and probably had done already. Men like Hussein commit the same sins over and over. Rebecca, for all her sophistication, had miscalculated. And where was he going home to? That's what I ask myself. Probably to his wife and his multiple children, all of them created in the image and spirit of their father.

Rebecca rallied in the presence of Dave. I have to commend her for her powers of recovery. As I walked with them down the road to the pub, I imagined that Rebecca could quite easily have set up a liaison whereby she might say she was going home, and then meet with Hussein in some other location, a little bistro perhaps or some boutique hotel. But judging by the forlorn look that I had seen on her face, I do not think that she was capable of being quite so devious. If anyone had a capacity for devious behaviour it was me. It is tempting to attribute one's own potential transgressions to others, but we are each of us unique, and deception can have many manifestations.

A merry little band had assembled in the pub. We kept adding chairs and squeezing ourselves in around the tables. It was quite jolly – like musical chairs with the liquor, but without the music. People got up to get their drinks or hurried to the Men's Room or to the Ladies, while others shifted their seats in order to be closer to the hub of the conversation. Bill relocated to go and talk politics to Julian, and left a space.

'Move over,' I said to Dave, and I wriggled into the gap and found myself wedged between Rebecca on one side and Monica on the other.

On the opposite side of the table, a glazed-looking Michael sat with a cigarette in one hand, a partly consumed glass of bitter in front of him. He grinned at me, turned very slightly red in the face and made a couple of aborted attempts to place the cigarette between his lips.

'What are you talking about?' I said.

Monica reckoned that Michael had drunk a whole bottle of burgundy by himself during the class, so he was not really talking about anything of a profound or coherent nature. Rebecca appeared not to hear this last statement. She explained that she had been making pronouncements about the deficiencies of the English male. One did not have to look far for examples. Michael took the cue and got up to go to the bathroom.

'There you are, you see, he's running away,' she said. She thought she had him cornered, but then I had arrived and he was gone. Rebecca started on me.

'Every time he talks to you he goes red,' was one of her lines, I remember. In truth I had not even had a chance to speak to him.

'What are you getting at, Rebecca?' I asked.

'Well, you know what you are doing, Sarah,' she said.

'What am I doing?'

'He always sits next to you,' she said.

'Yes?' I said.

'Well, you must realise what's happening.'

'No, what's happening?'

'He obviously likes you and you're encouraging him.'

'Rebecca,' I said, 'I only ever talk to him about the writing and the class.'

'You should keep off personal matters and just treat him as the teacher.'

'I do keep off personal matters. Anyway, I enjoy talking to him.'

I don't know why I said that. Michael did not have the appearance of someone who could be enjoyed. This conversation was beginning to disturb me. Who was Rebecca to tell me who I should be speaking to and about what? And why should this bother her anyway? What significance could it have? I really was at a loss.

'Has he got a reputation for this sort of thing?' I asked her.

'No, of course not,' she said.

'Oh, well, that's all right.'

Rebecca was going off on a three-week holiday to Cape Town, and good riddance to her I say, if she was going to tell people what to do and what not to do. I could imagine her telling Claire about me, and Claire grumbling, and then me being labelled as a troublemaker within the group: 'The woman who came to steal their tutor's heart.' Does this say something about me too? Do I purposely encourage men, and then reject them? Is that really me? Surely not! Michael tottered back, slumped into his seat and resumed his earlier grin. The evening proceeded more or less amicably after that.

It got close to seven and a few people started to get up to go. Opposite us, Michael stood up to put on his mac, and got into a terrible tangle, putting the wrong arm into the wrong hole. Monica put him right. I thought, Oh my God, there he goes again, totally lacking in style.

'Are you coming back to the class next term, Sarah?' he slurred, or was that just a speech defect?

'I'll have to see,' I said, 'I'm going to be away for a lot of the term. It's a great deal of money when you're not going to be there for half of the course.' A shade of concern passed across his face.

'It's a shame you're not coming to our dinner tomorrow night,' he said, half smiling, half smirking. I suspect his facial muscles had atrophied.

He and the rest of the men — except for one — departed in a body (safety in numbers) — home to join their wives and girlfriends I have no doubt. A small group of us — all women — remained. Dave hovered. We fell silent.

'Well, I'll be off then,' he said, and left.

Alone at last, we launched into our usual sharing of opinions, and the re-counting of past experiences. Monica told us of her trips to India and Turkey. I surprised myself by speaking knowledgably of the Japanese. I knew at least two members of this great nation. Muriel recalled African villages she had visited, and cures for amoebic dysentery. Rebecca warned us of fear and violence in

South Africa, and where the best theme resorts were to be found. Lindy told of her experiences in Italy, in Sardinia and then in Sicily. She spoke of a tour guide called Salvatore in Taormina. As I listened to this last account, my horror grew as I realised that her Salvatore near enough fitted the description of the Salvatore I had known – and later despised.

'I once knew a Salvatore,' I said. 'He was a tour guide too.'

'In Taormina?' said Lindy.

'Yes, and Catania. He sang a lot, I seem to remember.'

'That's the guy!' said Lindy. 'Had the most fabulous blue eyes! I tell you, he was to die for.'

No, I thought, I would not have died for him, but I might well have been tempted to murder him.

'Amazing!' said Rebecca who had followed these exchanges with the zeal of a tennis fan. 'Now the real coincidence,' she said, 'would be if you had both gone to bed with him!'

'I did,' said Lindy. 'Did you?'

I laughed. 'My goodness me, no,' I said, and we all laughed together, especially Rebecca.

Class Act II: Rebecca

So difficult to know what to wear. In the end, I decided on my violet and green silk scarf, the one I bought in a street market in Thailand. Gorgeous. Over a black tee-shirt. Very striking.

I was late leaving the house. I forgot the burgundy and having set the burglar alarm, I had to unset it and go back to retrieve the bottle. I dropped by the delicatessen on my way to the station and bought some tapas, and asked them to pop a couple of plastic forks in the package. I knew what they'd all be bringing – crisps and more crisps, Safeway's Family Pack. Spare me!

Someone rather smelly sat next to me on the tube, but surprisingly it didn't bother me too much. I simply got up and moved. I think I can say I was feeling quite buoyant. Getting rid of Sarah last week was a major coup. I really don't think she'll come this week. Claire and I were of like mind. She had to go. I don't know exactly what had upset Claire to fuel her little outburst against Sarah's male characters, but it seemed to work. Claire hates anyone coming in late when she's reading and Sarah is nearly always late, so I suppose it could have been a form of revenge. And anyway, Claire has a thing about male characters. The way they interact with the female characters in her stories is so … I don't know … ambiguous. It doesn't help that she slopes about looking depressed all the time. Perhaps she thinks that is the natural and most conducive state of mind for a writer? She's useful to have around, but she really should lighten up. I can't remember the last time she came with us to the pub.

Now that I think about it, who would want to sit drinking in a pub next to the Grim Reaper? I thought women's organisations were a thing of the past but she actually works for one, taking women's lib a haircut too far. Aren't I witty today?

As for Sarah, I'm sure she comes in late on purpose because she knows that Michael will save her the seat next to him. Does he think we hadn't noticed that he keeps his coat and briefcase on that chair for a reason?

I don't know what the matter is with Michael these days. Setting aside whatever is going on between him and Sarah, there's the question of the agent. I said to him two weeks ago, 'Michael, when is your agent coming to talk to us? You did promise, you know.' He mumbled something about her coming this week. I've been carrying this darned manuscript around with me for the past month and there's been no sign of the woman. If Michael doesn't produce her today, I can only think that he is demented and she's a figment of his imagination. Now, there's a thought. What if he doesn't have an agent at all? I have a list of questions as long as my arm that I want to ask her and she needs to see this manuscript. Admittedly it isn't complete, but what will she be expecting? Zadie Smith, Monica Ali? If she's worth her salt, she'll know good writing when she sees it.

I doubt that we'll do very much today. There'll be too much wine flowing for Michael to get any sense out of the class. The usual suspects will be there, I'm sure. That pompous fellow Bill, the builder and decorator; Alfred, who comes up from Hove; the old cleptomaniac who tried to slip one of my best leather gloves into her bag. I said to her, 'I think that's my glove you've got there,' and she said, 'Goodness me, where did that come from? I'm so terribly sorry'; the woman with the Turkish boyfriend; the skinny chap, the vegan, who works in the health food shop. I can't remember them all. Not a whole lot of talent there in any sense of the word. Oh, yes, and I'm forgetting that horrendous American woman who has a penchant for foreign waiters. She is so unbelievably loud.

I shall be very sorry if Hussein doesn't turn up. This is my last shot before we take a break. I've had time to suss him out. We're adults after all. We know the score. Sarah would never admit it, but she's had her eye on him since the beginning of term. All that playing hard to get. Maybe he's taken in by it, but it's fairly obvious to the rest of us.

What if she does turn up today? Worst case scenario. She makes eyes at Hussein and the two of them head off for a secret liaison. That would leave me Michael. He is not totally unattractive. Or failing him, there's Dave, but he's an unknown quantity. Something tells me I'd be scraping the bottom of the barrel.

I may be wrong but I'm pretty sure Michael is currently unattached. I heard on the college grapevine that he had had a big bust-up with Naomi. No idea why. Maybe she was envious of his success or he was envious of hers. Who knows?

But the more that I think about Sarah, the more irritated I become. God, that woman is infuriating, so 'holier than thou.' I could use all the clichés under the sun about her. She looks like butter wouldn't melt in her mouth. You'd think she was a nun – not interested in Hussein, not interested in Michael, not interested in men, presumably not interested in women either. Never been interested in anyone. Who the hell is she interested in?

Oh, if only … if only … if only there was something, some little transgression, some tiny tiny sin of the flesh, a microscopic peccadillo to indicate that she is just like us.

Class Act III: Dave

Today's the day. I'm going to make a move. I've thought about it long enough. It has to be today. It's the last day of term and everyone will be gone for the holiday, and some won't be coming back. That's what terrifies me. I've procrastinated, Lord knows, and now I stand to lose everything. If I don't act now, that could be the end of it. I wouldn't even be able to get in touch. I don't have a phone number, and how would I ever get one? Ask Michael? How would that sound? No, I have to sort it out myself – today.

Well, the good news is that she came. In the back of my mind I thought she might not after that tongue-lashing she took last week from those two bitches. To think that I'd given Rebecca some thought myself. She's attractive … very attractive, but she's pure poison. Any man can see that, even that arrogant bastard Hussein. He might try it on but if he does, he's going to find himself in shark-infested waters. My advice to him would be don't so much as dip in a toe. I saw him in the cafeteria before the class.

'That Rebecca, she's trouble,' he said.

I thought, good for him that he's got her worked out. 'Wouldn't touch her with a barge pole,' I said.

'But Sarah, she's a different matter.'

I thought I was going to choke. I pretended I didn't hear. I said, 'Anything planned for the weekend?'

'Yes, taking my wife and kids over to Hampstead. My sister's here from Iran and we're having a family get-together.' Then as an afterthought, he said, 'Must try not to eat too much. These women, they feed you up. Then they complain you're all out of shape.'

'Do you work out?'

'I'm pretty fit,' he said, 'I usually go after the class, unless I've got something more important on.' He gave me a wink. 'Got to get my priorities right.'

All that posturing and it turns out that Hussein isn't the great threat I thought him to be. I wasn't so sure about Michael until, well, I was carrying my coffee up to the class and Bill caught up with me on the stairs.

''Ere, 'ere,' he said. 'Never guess who I saw in Leicester Square with some bird?'

'Lay off,' I said. 'How many million people pass through Leicester Square every day?'

'Michael!' he hissed. 'I saw Michael with this woman.'

'Naomi,' I said.

'No, not Naomi!' He was adamant.

For a split second I thought, oh my God – Sarah.

'They were hand-in-hand, you know, snuggling up to each other, all smoochy. Probably off to some restaurant or other.'

I stopped on the stairs to look at him. It couldn't have been Sarah. He'd have said.

'So who was it?'

'That's what the break-up was about,' continued Bill. 'Naomi found out. Michael's been playing around … and then that Claire, she saw them.'

'Eh?' I said.

'Claire! Misery memoirs. You know.'

'Yes, I know Claire,' I said.

Just then, one half of a swing door opened on the landing and Michael came trudging up the stairs. Browbeaten, or was that my imagination?

'Bill,' he said. 'Dave.' He hardly looked at us.

'Afternoon, Michael,' I said. 'See you shortly.'

'All right, Michael?' said Bill.

We stood in silence until Michael had reached the other landing and was out of earshot.

Bill continued, whispering. 'Claire works over that way – Leicester Square. She knows Naomi through the women's group. And it was Claire, see, who told Naomi.'

There's me, standing on the stairs, burning my fingers on the coffee cup, looking completely blank. I was completely blank. I was at a loss.

I said, 'So, who was it then?'

'Who was what?' said Bill.

'Who was the woman smooching around with Michael in Leicester Square?'

'Kate!' he said. 'It was Kate. The bird from the literary agency. The one who's supposed to be coming today.'

'Oh,' I said.

'Kate was Naomi's agent. Get it?'

'Oh,' I said. I didn't know if I was getting it or not. I was thinking that that was probably how Michael got most of his stuff published – through Naomi, only temptation got the better of him. He had a little help from his friends, and he had more help from some friends than from others. That wasn't fair, was it?

'Oh,' I said again.

'Yeah!' said Bill, looking very pleased with himself.

That was that then. I didn't reckon we'd be seeing Kate ... ever. Michael was in the dog house, out of favour with Naomi because of Kate. And Kate was out of a job because of Michael, asked to leave the agency, conflict of interests or something. It's all a complete disaster. I'll have to buy the guy a beer. What this means... what this really means is that Sarah's fair game. No excuses. Go get her, Dave. I'd be an idiot not to. Today's the day ... and tonight's the night. I mean, who'd have thought this is how it would turn out?

Ten Ways You Changed Me

I HAVE SO much to thank you for. I was all wrong, flawed. But you changed me. You made me better. Before you, I didn't work – the brain, the thoughts, the actions – none of these worked. But now all of that's changed. You remember how I was so disorderly? I'd drop my clothes on the floor, or throw them over the back of a chair. But you changed all that. You said, 'Take care of your things and they'll last.' I hadn't given the lasting much thought, but after that I could see what you were getting at. There's no need for something new, no need for replacements – is there? – when your originals can do the job. You didn't waste your money buying me gifts. You didn't need to. I could look after my own things by myself.

From you, I learned the practicalities of life. I was young, of course. I came to you fresh and untutored. You shaped me. You formed me. You taught me humility. Before you there was an arrogance about me. I was disrespectful. When we walked together, I looked about me, my head held high. I caught the attention of other men. I looked them boldly in the eye. I did that then. But I learned from you that this was not your way. I learned to avert my gaze, to cast down my eyes. For you knew that any other way would lead me into error, and this is what I came to understand.

This way I had of displaying myself. You saw that and you put me right. You held me close and you told me how you could make me better. And you'll remember as I do how you slowly and deliberately wiped my mouth clean of lipstick. I was false and I became true again. In the mirror I saw myself as I really was. I found the real me, the one who did not hide behind a façade. I came to understand better how others saw me, how they might have misinterpreted me. I found an honesty that I did not have before, thanks to you.

You taught me the value of friendships, that there are people in our lives we do not need. There were many people who were drawn to me in those early days, friends who sought out my company. The phone rang often. There were invitations, groups of friends who arrived unannounced, happy to pass time in my company, urging me to join them. But you'll remember how they distanced themselves when they met you. My time, in any case, was yours. Those people excluded themselves and were excluded. But you explained to me how, in the long term, this was for my own good. For people, you said, have a way of taking you over.

And so it was that I learned to be alone, to hold the space, to wait. For, you'll remember that I waited for you. Night after night. You came when you were free. I knew your life was full in the way that many men's lives are full and I accepted that I was only the tiniest part of your life. The waiting was hard, but from you I learned patience.

What else? For there are so many things of yours that changed me. Trust. Yes, trust. You taught me what it was like to trust and be trusted. Do you remember that time when you came to me in the dead of night, asking me to keep for you a heavy metal box? You told me to trust you. You told me not to look inside but, of course, I did. I was changed by you, but not entirely. In the box, I saw those three handguns. Why would you have needed weapons? That I didn't ask. What was it that I didn't know or understand about you and your life? You said, 'Don't look,' but I knew you wanted me to. And it was after that that I got you to show me how to load and fire one of your guns, and I saw that it made you happy. You said, 'Look. Pay attention. You don't mess with firearms. You lift, you aim, you squeeze and that is how it's done.' And you explained to me that there are times when we may need to take action. And, when those times come, we must not hesitate. We must do what we need to do as and when we need to do it. So, when you slept tonight, I took a gun and I pressed the barrel against your forehead and I squeezed the trigger and I closed my eyes, remembering all the things you said and did to change me.

⊷⬤ ⬤⊶

The Older Short-Haired Female

She was the older, short-haired female. A rather aggressive species, he thought. Older, and therefore experienced. It was fearsome for him to consider – and so he did not – the lives she had lived, might have lived, lives she had enjoyed and destroyed, the wiliness of her moves directed by her knowledge of things past and carried forward now into the future.

He had spotted her from afar, blue-winged and scarlet in her habitat, a high-flying estuary bird of a kind he had rarely observed before.

He should have known better. The older, short-haired female is not to be meddled with. Not by the likes of him. She fluttered seductively in men's paths, knowing what she knew and applying it to her advantage. Unlike the past, when she had applied it to her disadvantage. For she had once been the prey of man. Easy prey. But then she was the younger, long-haired female, a delicate, pale creature, verging on the anorexic, easy to have, easy to please, easy to leave and take another.

Now she was a more evolved specimen, not as sleek perhaps, weathered – maybe hardened – possibly, but also, and resoundingly, magnetic, compulsive, charismatic, alluring, luring the helpless man-beast to her nest, entrapping and entangling the hopeless, hapless male in his inevitable flight towards an un-defined fulfilment. But with one certainty: that once ensnared, he was never to escape. As surely as the sparrow hawk preyed on smaller birds, who ate the grubs in the earth, who ate the nutrients of the soil, the older, short-haired female played her part in the chain of man's downfall, but perhaps also his redemption.

94

She sits at a mirror, a distant captive behind the wrought iron bars of her balcony. He watches her, captivated. She lifts her brush and pulls it carefully through glistening plumage. She turns her face this way and that, staring into her reflection. He experiences a private ecstasy, reserved for secret observers. Viewing her in silence, his home a hide with slits and peep holes, his home a hive of excited anticipation, as her robe floats feather-like to the carpet, he knows he must have her. And, when her silhouette slips from view, his hand caresses the curved inanimate surfaces of stolen eggs on the rich polished wood of the dresser in his bedroom, and he believes himself all powerful, a licensed thief of nature.

You must not move about or make a noise.
This is not conducive to the intimate study of birds.

It is a long-term project. He observes her habits, notes her displays. He knows little of her mating patterns, but he waits. He prepares himself for her broody promiscuity, knowing that it will disappoint him. Such is the species, but his is a scientific approach. He always bases action on careful research. When action is necessary, he takes it.

He passes her on the stairs. She looks at him, but does not see. He nods his head in acknowledgement. Her coat brushes his. She is there and, with a faint rustle, she is gone. He hears the door close behind her.

A case history. He watches and takes note. She is totally self-centred, an arrogant, intimidating creature. All the more intriguing for this. He observes. She preens herself with conviction and commitment.

You must always take care to keep your distance.

She is in her kitchen. She takes something from a cupboard. She turns her head and inclines it, as if listening. She stands immobile. She moves to the window. She pulls down the blind.

*You, of all people, must comprehend the problems facing wild birds, the
threats to their environment, the violation of their natural habitats.*

Field observation. She is unlocking her car. She looks up as he passes. He would
like to see her at close hand. He needs to know what she is like, her behaviour.
The older, short-haired female always stands her ground. She stares you right in
the eye. He lowers his eyes and moves on.

*There are many ways to attract wild birds, but these methods cannot
be relied upon. Frequently birds are heard but not seen.
As you must certainly know, they often appear when least expected.*

He stands behind the door in the darkness of his hall. There is a circular mark-
ing of light around his eye. He watches her through his spy hole as she waits for
his response to her call. He notes her restlessness and this gives him pleasure.
She rings the bell, but he does not answer. He knows she will return. She will
come closer and closer... until she is close enough to touch. He will wait and
watch. He knows his chance will come.

'I live across the courtyard,' she tells him.

    'Ah, yes,' he says.

    'I wondered if I might...'

    'Of course,' he says.

    Good fortune and a rapport with birds have brought her to him. He is mas-
terful with birds. Silently he listens as she reports the fault from the phone in
his study.

*You believe in conservation. Beware. The conservation of memory and
desire belongs only to human-kind. It is folly to seek in others what you
find in yourself.*

'Your glove,' he says.

'I never missed it,' she tells him. What she loses – or has lost – is of no consequence to her.

Yes, he will accept a drink.

He stands in her living room. He has never seen this room before. It is not within his range.

The bird is an unpredictable creature. You cannot be sure how it may react when threatened. Take care not to alarm it.

Her flight is late.

'I hope you won't think me rude,' he says, as he stands in her doorway. 'I've cooked enough for two.'

He has always shown a concern for the protection and welfare of the wild bird.

She is glad of the offer.

The light is dimmed. She perches on a stool in his kitchen. She pecks at her food, watching him. He offers her food from his own plate. Just a taste. If she will.

She will.

She grasps his hand in hers. Her nails are long and polished. She takes the food with her teeth and tongue. She is lit by the candlelight. Her eyes glint, her pupils wide and dark. His fingertips stretch towards the transparent down of eyebrows, and then to the soft pink of her lips.

'I have her,' he thinks. 'I have... her.'

And one, or the other, is captivated.

He wakes in the half-light of the morning. There is a distant electric dawn. She is an early bird, humming as she splashes under his shower. He hears her voice and closes his eyes. He feels her presence in the room, an emperor and his nightingale. She rustles close by. In his dream, he turns to watch her as she bends towards the telescope. She speaks softly.

'A perfect view,' she says, 'perfect,' and her words dissolve into melodious, singing laughter. He smiles in his sleep.

Light floods his room. On the floor there is crushed eggshell, but it hardly matters. He views her through his binoculars and knows she will see him. Is this wise? She is speaking on the phone. She turns, catches sight and waves to him. She is smiling. He waves back. He is, of course, a tamer of wild birds.

'I'll be away. A day or two,' she says when he calls.

'I'll miss you,' he says.

'I'll miss you too.'

Generally, birds do not display their emotions.

He knows this, but he has forgotten.

'I'll call you,' she tells him. 'Or you call me.'

He goes about his business. Common birds are dots in the distance, looking dark and colourless. They hardly interest him. She is his obsession now. He is aware that the migratory bird is at risk abroad and this troubles him. At his office he waits to be called, but his phone is silent. He calls her.

'You're back,' he says.

Yes, she's back.

Perhaps his feeling for birds has failed him.

But she is joyful. She longs to be with him. She says.

'We'll see each other soon,' she says. 'Call me. Any time. Day or night.'

These creatures come and go airily. They snatch what they can. They are erratic. They flit here and there. They swoop, they steal, they mislead. They are elusive. They soar out of reach. They abandon you.

Being an expert in the field does not equip you to manage it.
You have been, and were intended to be, an observer, not a participator.

He trains his telescope on her windows. Her shutters are closed.

He calls her. The answering machine engages, and he hears her voice. The sullen, serious voice of the older, short-haired female.

'Leave a message,' the voice tells him.

Leave a thought, an aspiration, a fear? He cannot abide his words gliding on this limbo of airways.

You must surely remember the raptors.
There is a link through time, forgotten
or ignored as desires replace wisdom, as greed cancels caution.
When handling predators, you must mind the talons.

He thinks on these matters as he waits, illuminated only by his hallway's prehistoric glow. Across the courtyard, her shutters open. It takes him by surprise. He focuses the lenses. She faces him directly. Her arm is raised. She is pointing, identifying him to others – to the men standing by her side. Waiting to spot him.

And then comes the moment when, in its impotence,
as beating wings descend,
the prey is paralysed by the cognizance of its fate.

⸺⬝⬝⬝⸺

Needled

It was bitterness drove me to it.

>Over the phoneline, he gave pathetic, tortured little squeals.
>'What's the matter?'
>'I've got terrible pains in my legs.'
>'Like burning?'
>'Burning, stabbing.'
>'Like serrated skewers grinding through the muscle tissue?'
>'Yes.'

He'd go into great, whining detail about how agonising it was, about what his physiotherapist said, about how badly it was affecting him and so on.

>'Mmm, poor you. Oh dear.'

I had another strange dream last night. It was unpleasant, a bit sour. Someone visited me. Maybe a police officer. At first I thought he was calling about my car. But this man had the air of it being about something much more serious. He wanted a space where we could talk. Somewhere private, he said. I suggested an unoccupied table, but there were lots of people milling about in the vicinity. I've no idea what they were doing in our house. The table was rectangular, like our wooden kitchen table at home, with cuts and ridges in it. Over the top of it was a plastic covering. It crinkled when you put down a piece of paper and wrote on it. The policeman was in plain clothes with butter from the tabletop staining his sleeves. He didn't look best pleased. He put something down in front of me.

It was an ebony chess piece, and it had needles sticking out of it.

'So,' he said, 'what else have you done?'

My Friend Eric

I SAW HIM at the far end of the shop. My friend Eric. He looked much as he had done the last time I saw him, with his hair wild and grey about his face, his beard broad and frizzy, his features the same as before. No changes for Eric. A new jacket perhaps.

I knew enough about Eric as I needed to know. It wasn't important to know if he was rich or poor or what he did, or if he had a job or a girlfriend. I knew I could ring him up at any time.

'It's me,' I'd say. 'What are you doing tonight, Eric?' It was no use asking Eric about next week. He couldn't plan for tomorrow, let alone next week. Eric lived for the day. If he was free, he was free. If he was busy, then he had a date... a girl to bed, a friend to stay, visitors from abroad to entertain. Eric was the sort of person who could come out at a moment's notice. That's why we got on so well. He'd never call me. He just waited to be called. He was undemanding, and that's what I liked about him. And now here he was, wandering through the perfume department, his hands in his pockets, a faraway look in his eyes.

Once he had brought me a present.

'What's this?' I said.

'A shampoo,' he said.

'What made you bring me that?' I said.

He shrugged. 'Might come in handy,' he said.

'Thanks,' I said, and stuffed the sachet into my pocket. We were art students then, or rather I was the student. He was the model. Eric had nothing to hide from me. I never used the shampoo. It was depilatory cream.

'Trying to make me go bald, Eric?' I said. He didn't believe me when I told him. He was mortified.

'Sorry,' he said. 'I hadn't realised. Anyway,' he said, 'it's the thought that counts.'

Eric was thoughtful all right. There was no doubt about that. He always brought me something. Sometimes it was food, an avocado sandwich or a couple of nectarines, or a pineapple, or a chocolate bar or some bubble gum. He brought me the strangest of things. I didn't use aftershave or take throat lozenges or milk of magnesia, but I looked forward to his gifts and I took them in good part, even the two-pronged plugs and the packets of fruit-flavoured Durex.

'Well, you never know when they'll come in handy,' said Eric. That was what he always said.

Eric turned to face me. We were still some distance apart. He looked directly ahead. I guessed he had seen me. I walked towards him and, as I did, his arm reached out independently of the rest of his body and, with a pincer-like movement, his hand captured a large bottle of perfume displayed on the counter to his right. With a rapid flick of the wrist, the bottle was sunken into the depths of his voluminous pocket. He saw me. I saw him, and we both stopped in our tracks.

'Flocky!' he said. 'How you doin'?'

'The coffee's on me,' I said as we reached the cafe. It was a favourite place of his. He had taken me there the evening I'd told him of my infatuation with the exotic Francisco.

'He's no good for you,' he told me. 'Anyway, he's a Leo. They're vain,' he said. 'You bark at them and they run a mile. You're wasting your time with a man like that.' Eric knew exactly how to give advice to women. 'I've been telling you for years,' he said, 'you ought to come to bed with me. You'd have the time of your life.'

Maybe I would have, but he knew, and I knew, that it would have been the end of a perfect friendship.

'So, what've you been up to?' he asked me.

I wanted to ask the same question. 'I've got a new job,' I said.

'Good,' he said.

'That's why I haven't been in touch. What about you?'

'Same as ever,' he said. 'A bit of this. A bit of that.'

'A bit of nicking,' I said.

'Aw, come on,' he said. 'You know me.'

'I'm not sure that I do.' I felt a bit put out.

'I can take care of myself,' he said.

There was a moment of silence between us as I watched the waitress delivering pastries at the next table, and as Eric eyed two girls speaking in French over my shoulder.

'What's this new job, then?' he said.

'In a shop.'

'In a shop?' He wasn't that impressed. I could tell. 'What do you do?'

'Well,' I said. 'I'm ...'

'Yeah?' he said.

'I'm a store detective.'

Crime–Dating

For the sake of his art, Bernardo was going to have to murder someone. Up to now he had believed he could only write what he knew. He was a university professor and that meant he knew many things, but not how to murder someone. As he considered all of this, he moved slowly around the room, tea cup in hand, looking at the framed images on the walls. In one, a man lay face down in a puddle of blood with a white rose placed on the back of his jacket between his shoulder blades. In another, a woman stood sideways on against a darkened wall, in her hand a gun, the barrel of which she pressed against her cheek. In a third … Bernardo stumbled. His notepad slipped from under his arm, and his cup toppled in its saucer.

There had been a collision of sorts. The woman who faced him, and who now wiped droplets of tea from her shirt, was evidently displeased.

'I'm so awfully sorry,' said Bernardo. 'I didn't see you.'

'Not seeing people can get you into a lot of trouble,' said the woman.

'Can it?' said Bernardo. 'And why is that?'

'Because,' said the woman, 'the people you don't see and that you walk into and over, get enraged and then …' She paused.

'And then?'

'And then they kill you. As I'm sure you must know, it's one of the most popular themes of crime fiction: revenge.'

'So, are you saying that as a result of my walking into you, you might become enraged and murder me?'

'If I were so inclined, then yes,' said the woman.

'And are you?' said Bernardo.

'I suppose I am annoyed that you didn't see me. It suggests that I may be of no consequence.'

'Well, effectively, you are of no consequence to me though, admittedly, you may well be of consequence to someone else.'

'Lucky me,' said the woman.

Bernardo held out his hand. 'Bernardo,' said Bernardo.

'Bernardo what?' said the woman.

'Bianco,' said Bernardo.

'Eleanor Sikorski,' said the woman. 'You may have heard of me.'

'No,' said Bernardo.

Eleanor frowned. 'And what brings you here today, Bernardo?' she said.

It seemed to Bernardo that he studied the woman a long time before answering. She was of pleasing appearance, decidedly Anglo-Saxon, not his usual type, but she might be. In women, his taste was eclectic. But why had he allowed himself to be drawn into a conversation that put him at such a distinct disadvantage? Who was she to challenge him? Who was she to oblige him to answer? For he did feel obliged to answer. He stooped and retrieved his notebook.

Eleanor waited, her head cocked slightly to one side. Bernardo opened his mouth to speak.

'Yes?' she said.

'I am here by accident,' said Bernardo.

'I see,' said Eleanor. 'You're here by accident at the Hampstead CrimeFest.'

Bernardo brushed a lock of hair from his eyes. 'I had to come,' he said. 'A friend gave me a ticket and I didn't want to offend him.'

'Ah, I understand,' she said. 'You're not planning fictional murders. You're just killing time.'

'Yes,' said Bernardo.

'So, why are you taking notes?'

'I was writing my shopping list,' said Bernardo. He held out his notepad for her to see.

Eleanor blinked at the page, then looked at Bernardo.

Bernardo gave her a self-satisfied smile. 'I always write notes to myself in Italian,' he said.

'You won't be able to buy any of those things in a shop,' said Eleanor.

Bernardo felt a hot flush come over him. 'You read Italian?'

'*Sì*,' said Eleanor.

The Hampstead CrimeFest café, unlike the hospitality lounge, served grey-coloured coffee in polystyrene cups, but the digestive biscuits were nice.

'Have another biscuit,' said Eleanor. 'They're English and homemade, and they'll do you good.'

'Are you also here by accident?' asked Bernardo.

'No, I have already found my true path,' said Eleanor. 'However, it took some time. I am a novelist. I came here today to talk about the Foreign-Detective Protagonist. Did you come to my talk?'

'No,' said Bernardo.

'So, you haven't heard of me, and you didn't come to my talk.'

'No,' said Bernardo, reaching for another biscuit. 'What's your day job?'

'I am a novelist. That *is* my day job. And what is *your* day job?'

'I am also a novelist,' said Bernardo. 'I'm quite well known. There was an article about me recently in one of the Sunday supplements.'

Eleanor's eyes seemed to flicker, a tiny light of admission, of begrudging acceptance. 'I only read the Guardian Saturday Review,' she said.

'I can't believe that,' said Bernardo.

Eleanor cleared her throat. 'Well, sometimes I read the supplements.'

'Did you read this one?'

'Yes, I suppose I might have.'

'I think you did read it,' said Bernardo, 'and I think you remember it very well.'

'If I did read, then I will have to refresh my memory.'

Bernardo's phone gave a beep. He checked his message. It read: 'Join us this weekend at the Jingle Bells Play Emporium – special offers for all seasons.'

'My publisher,' said Bernardo. He stood up. 'I'm afraid I shall have to go. Would you care to resume this conversation over lunch and a glass of wine?'

Eleanor's expression, he noted, was somewhere between envy and awe.

That afternoon, as Bernardo drove back to W11, he revelled in the joy of one-upmanship.

Skin Deep

1

Skin Deep

1.1 In my life, there was a new man. My hopes for him were great. In the secrecy of my thoughts, I would investigate him. Could he sense it? As he slept in his own sheets, in the privacy of his own home, I touched and caressed him and urged him to do to me all the delights I wished for myself. Would he ever know the power of my dreaming mind as it dismantled and then re-constructed him? And sometimes I wondered if, when the real man awoke, he would suffer the fatigue of that night spent in my arms, in the warmth of my bed, in the heat of my unrelenting imagination. In the cold light of day I asked myself, as honestly as I was ever capable of asking myself, if this man would fulfil the perfection I demanded of him? I knew he would not. But then I realised that I, too, could never fulfil the perfection I demanded of myself. And this I knew with absolute certainty.

1.2 Here I was, a woman condemned from birth to live a life of imperfection. I was – and would have been – perfect, except for my defects. Perhaps this man would desire me, want me momentarily, but it was more likely that he would not. I was an impostor, appearing as one thing, while really another. I would be discovered at some point soon. He would discover, to his infinite horror, that the woman he had desired was wholly and horribly imperfect. Worse still, the discovery would take place at the moment of seduction. Little wonder then that I chose to control my lovers through the pages of my book and the colours of my mind. Yet, always the novelty of a fresh, unbiased lover drew me. Surely, I told myself, I could not account for the diversity of men's taste. Imperfection to one might mean satisfaction to another. If a man rated loyalty and purity above physical qualities, I was indeed perfect. I was by merit of my imperfection, I admit, virtually untouched. Virtually. Not entirely.

1.3 I would never be quite up to standard, I would never totally make the grade, and therefore, I deduced, I would never be entirely like other women. The man seeking normality would cast me out into a world void of the emotions I sought. An artificial impostor of a woman, I looked at myself, unloved and neglected, in my bedroom mirror, wondering if somewhere there might be a man, equally imperfect, who would have me. There was a slight darkening of the pale skin beneath my eyes. In the half-light of the morning, the darkness menaced me. My hair stood shrub-like around my ears, surprised by my early rising. My eyes shone glassily into my reflection. My breath hung bitter in my mouth. I considered it a great misfortune that the woman I longed to see in the mirror evaded me. Who was the man who would have me? Who would accept me as I was? Who was the man who would go to the seconds shop and buy the goods stamped imperfect? Surely I would not want such an undiscerning man?

1.4 Would he not, in any case, return me with his receipt when he found an item that better matched his requirements? And this, indeed, was the way of all men. I knew it. There had been many other women returned, replaced by better models. But some, doll-like, were perfect from the outset. How could they be born into such perfection? They were from every angle satisfactory, pleasing, and even delightful, to the eye. No re-touching necessary, no artificial aids or strange devices. No techniques applied to re-model or re-shape, no diets or taking in a pinch or two here or there. Just pure natural constant beauty, rising in the morning with no bodily odours or panda rings beneath the eyes or bags or coughs or explosions of evil gases. Creatures who have no machinery or chemical workings within their bodies. They slip silkily into soft garments. Slink to their coffee cups. Sip, and one sip is enough. No turgid liquids needed to coat their crystal skin. Just the natural pink glow to glint across the breakfast table at their lovers.

1.5 How fortunate the man, how cruel in his judgement and in his demands, forever excluding the imperfect such as me. Could I improve? Could I maintain the deception of perfection? I could try. But I had always tried, knowing that the story would end as it had always done, with my rejection of him, with his rejection of me, and a long and perfect loneliness until the next love took me. I always fell in love in November and, as destiny's order often decreed, I would fall out of love, an intense and deep infatuation, a torturous striving for perfection, after a month, or a year, or two, or even three, but always in the month of December. Thus my Christmases were vacant, winter walks and aimless shopping days, or dreamful afternoons of blissful hopes and invented futures, but always alone, always in loneliness, in solitude. And now, once again, I fulfilled my own prophesies of isolation.

2

Skin Deeper

2.1 My new lover, who sought perfection and found merely the substitute in me, had already discovered its true essence in a real woman. It was with her, this genuine article, that he chose to divide his festive time. Later he would return to me, the imitation that I was, and I would welcome him. It would be a homecoming, a joyous occasion of much eating, and of drinking wine and champagne. Then he would be gone. And I would repair my marred features, comb the much ruffled and tangled hair, smooth the crumpled and beaten sheets, wash the plates and cutlery and glasses. And if all this was to be done, and to be done as carefully and as tidily as possible, and if the sweeping of the battlefield demanded much of me, and it did, I wondered not just of my physical imperfection, but also of my mental and spiritual defects. I was, and again I acknowledged it sorrowfully and honestly, to myself, just not good enough. The woman who lived in my lover's house, the woman who warmed his bed, soothed his dreams and calmed his fevers, how secure and confident she must be.

2.2 How efficiently, how matter-of-factly she must go about her business. Deftly she would disperse clutter, she would clean perspirationlessly, she would throw vegetables with strange-sounding names into heavy, expensive pans to produce exotic and erotic suppers for her weary lover home from work. My mind and my heart wept at this knowledge of my rival: she who glowed with a warmth to her skin, a natural rosiness to her lips, a radiant gloss to her hair, a luminous sparkle to her eyes. All else enhancement. My soul filled with sorrow for the presence of this woman who now, in the casualness of her intimacy, readied herself for the day with the merest slick of lipstick, with a feather-light dusting of the faintest of powder. It pained me, this thought. And, imperfect as I was, I wished in my heart and body that I could be as equally perfect. To have the same hair, the same skin, the same complexion, the same energies and skills, the same competence and intelligence as my most fortunate rival.

2.3 Even in my imperfection, I harboured hope. I would transform or be transformed. No longer myself but another, a more highly valued and privileged other. Slowly I would slip into place and replace. Men, in their ignorance, were poor discriminators, women like flavours to their taste buds. Salty today, but sweet tomorrow. Would he, my lover, deny me still if I perfectly matched the other? Each mirror I passed in the dimness and the silence of my house reflected back my unworthiness, my same skin and eyes and hair, worked and re-worked. My face was a landscape, I was an explorer. Every day a new discovery of creeks and crevasses where none had been before, new areas of arid waste and untamed swamps of murky oiliness. In the dawn light I laboured to conceal my blotched and blemished countenance. I added tone and vitality where there was none. I discovered and drew my hidden lips. Half tone became colour, whites to tan, greys to pinks. Diligently I worked at my daily metamorphosis. And on and on with a treadmill of a life of correcting, repairing and improving, to become human, to meet the world, to become one of its kind. Soon I would fit, and be fitting.

2.4 Now in the harsh light of day I stood corrected and improved. My mirrors shone. Glints of light reflected adjustments to my errors of conformation. Lumpy surfaces were masked, spiky skin smoothed, the puffiness of knees hidden. Curlers, correctors, pots and tubes, brushes and sponges consigned to their secret places, far from the evaluating eye. And cast a spell I would upon my lover, a spell of impaired and hazy vision, protection against too close a scrutiny and flawful discoveries. I earned praiseful words and flatteries for what I was, for what I had become, for what I had made myself. But I rejected them all, for they were not worthy of me. I scorned, I ignored, I withdrew, admired from afar by many, loved by no-one, least of all myself. In his street, beneath his illuminated window, in dark security, I waited to glimpse my lover hurry home. A momentary sighting, a vision through the steamy pane of my windscreen as he scurried, umbrella waving damp greetings in the rain to the woman who watched from the window above.

2.5 And from below, I caught only snatches of the ebony hair and the woman's swift, efficient movements. I bit my lip and restrained my tears at the thought of this rival, so much better than I was. This was the woman who shared my lover's sparkling conversation, his charm, his romance, his soft and loving voice, his touch, the moisture of his lips, the earnestness of his gaze, the gentle rhythm of his breath, his sighs and – I stared longingly and bitterly through the condensation – his ecstasy. I owned all these things too, but only in part. I rented them. They were on hire. I did not own him. He was not mine wholly. I did not have his heart. I had him only temporarily, for brief though sometimes intense moments, but only momentarily because I did not qualify, I did not pass, or merit a greater or a more permanent share. What was, then, the secret of perfection and, through perfection, the attainment of his desire? How could I learn? When would I be worthy? How was I to earn my prize? And when the lights dimmed and the lovemaking began, late, very late into the night, I drove home through the rain, tears on my cheeks, pathetic, wretchedness within and without.

3

Skin Deepest

3.1 Now here I was again in his house. His invitations were rare. Each visit, I thought, would be the last. He feared, I supposed, for tell-tale clues to my presence, an errant smudge of make-up on newly laundered towels. My fingers traced across the objects on his shelves and sideboards. Small metallic objects in blacks and greys, white wood picture frames, cupboards of ash wood and glass, porcelain objects cold within their cases, books, record collections tightly packed, ordered and regimented. It was a house of no colour, but of exquisite elegance. It was a glossy photo on a coffee table. It was greys and silvers, and blacks and whites, charcoal drawings and colourless watercolours, a house of memorials and past things and ages, and another world that was not my own, but which I desired nonetheless. I saw myself, and yet could not see myself, there in the house. My image of myself flickered and failed even as I willed it to remain. The woman I imagined into each of those rooms was impaired. I did not match or blend. But the other, in her perfection, did.

3.2 The woman's neat little frame, her dainty, bird-like figure, her delicate and fragile limbs. This other woman, his chosen one, was right and exact and correct. She matched. She fitted. The house was truly hers as it was his. And I wondered if this woman ever brought warmth to this house, and colour and sound, for music played, but there was no melody that I could remember. And as my fingers slid across the shiny surface of the wood, they met the icy metal of an ornate silver frame, and inside the frame, their photo together. A field, a grassy area of colourless green, two small figures in isolation. His arm, linked inside the woman's, his face widened in an uncharacteristic joyous smile turned towards hers, and her face half hidden by her dark hair, so distant and small a face that it was impossible to define or evaluate. For judge I must, and compare myself with that other woman. I lifted the frame and studied the picture, though I could learn nothing more than I had already imagined, and that was painful and destructive and it corroded my heart. Replacing the photograph, a rectangular card fluttered down onto the cream-piled carpet and rested at my feet. I stooped to retrieve it.

3.3 In my hands, the gold-edged card with black, shiny words embossed on its smooth white surface, an announcement, an invitation to an event that was of importance only in that it opened another door to a world alien to mine, within which their lives intertwined with the lives of others, their names written in an entangled script, as they were wrought in this private life of theirs, identified and recognised as two people welded together, specially and expertly constructed solely for each other. So, now I was here in his home, experiencing, as he did, a confinement of sights and sounds and smells within a senseless environment, and it meant nothing to me, only that one woman qualified to live with him and one did not. And the one who did was far better than the one who did not. And I wrote and I wrote, and the words curled about the pages and wove in and out of themselves, sometimes happily, almost always sadly, and they had no true destination but my very own heart. The thoughts of passion past and the barren present took hold of my words and made them cast themselves violently upon the expanse of whiteness, staining it with their truth and their imaginings. The time was come to judge and to compare, measure and evaluate.

3.4 I stood, luminous amidst a mingling of unexceptional faces, no invitation, no gold-edged card, a presentable intruder, a lone woman, threatening an anxiety of wives and tempting an excitement of husbands. Who would dare to challenge me, an impostor who was so forthright in her own presence, so striking in her individuality? Observing, analysing, waiting, I scanned the hum for his voice until, with a stab of exhilaration, I heard him. I saw him, this man I had created in my mind, but who existed as another. I saw him printed on a green landscape, a protective cluster of acquaintances chattering noiselessly around him. And at his side, as ordained by my imagination, superb and superior, there was indeed a far better person than me, a woman of considerable magnificence. Here in life this woman assumed a far greater stature than I had ever imagined. The fears and suppositions I had embraced, the beliefs and prophecies, were now fulfilled and confirmed as if in one overwhelming tidal wave of cruel and inevitable betrayal.

3.5 I turned away in avoidance of my own distress and, in my grief, I met with a tiny creature, lank-haired and sparrow-like who, with the silent touch of a falling leaf, brushed past me, lightly, efficiently. Something held me, a transitory enchantment, the faintest memory recalled, the slightest thought remembered. Turning back, I glimpsed that unmistakable linking of arms. I recognized the dull, dark eyes cast upwards towards his, and his gaze, radiating down onto this his lover's meek and sallow skin, uncovered now in its immutable and eternal plainness.

> *Plain, like the early winter sky.*
> *Plain, like the soil of the earth.*
> *Plain, like the paint on the wall.*
> *Plain, like the water from a tap.*

Thus it was that this chapter like the others closed, so I might now live with this man only on the pages of his book, not mine. For, in my perfection, and in my imperfection, he did not merit me. But, then, who did?

⇥ ⇤

Tooth

HE KNEW HE had to say something, but he didn't know how. He watched Amy as she milled about the kitchen organizing, preparing, jangling pots and pans. He watched as she poured out his tea.

'You're very quiet this evening,' she said, placing the mug on the table in front of him. 'Something the matter?'

'No,' he said. He felt his fingers twitch. He gave an approximation of a smile. Something reassuring, he thought.

Amy moved away and continued about her business. She opened cupboards, rummaged inside them, shut them.

The more he looked at her, the more he decided he wanted to find fault with her, but as yet he hadn't decided what that fault was. It wasn't the way she moved, or what she wore or what she did, but it was something he would think of soon. He stirred his tea, drank it slowly and tasted only guilt.

The fact was that he had tired of her. The fact was that Sharon was back in his life. These were the facts. There was no room now for Amy. She was extra. If he had known that Sharon was going to take him back, he wouldn't have got involved with Amy. Or maybe he would have anyway. His question to himself was … had he got himself involved with Amy? Had he insinuated himself into her life and broken something that didn't need fixing? As a salesman, he was good at what he did, but hadn't he sold Amy something she really hadn't needed? Hadn't Amy been perfectly fine before he stepped into her life? He stirred his tea and watched a single tea leaf spin on its surface. Now he knew he must set aside all this agonizing and do the right thing. Just tell her. The telling comes easier if there is a reason. He studied her again, looked at her face. And then he got it.

It was the tooth. That awful front tooth of hers that wedged out over her lower lip every time she smiled. How could he ever live with that? How had he lived with that tooth up to now? Why hadn't she got her teeth fixed like other women and set that tooth back where it belonged? There was something inexplicably repulsive about it. Why it had not been repulsive three months back, he did not know, but it suited him now to accuse that tooth.

'What is it?' she said. She had turned to see him gazing at her. 'Something's wrong, isn't it?' She was stopped in the middle of the kitchen, dishcloth in hand.

'Yes,' he said.

She blinked.

He noted the slight depression the tooth made on her lower lip. He had made the right decision. 'I don't love you anymore,' he said.

'What?' she said.

He stood up, picked up his coat and keys, and walked towards the door. 'Sorry,' he said.

He left her standing there, pale and stunned, in the middle of the kitchen.

He stepped out into the street and felt the rush of cold night air on his face. He felt the relief of it. Elation, but at the same time a desire to run, to escape and not to be accountable. He fumbled with his coat, pushing his arms into the sleeves like an ungainly child. In the dark, he did not see that the toe of his shoe was about to catch on the edge of a wayward paving stone just two strides from the front door of the house. He saw the concrete slabs rush up to meet his face. His entangled hands could not save him. He opened his mouth and he heard himself cry out. He felt his front teeth crack with the full weight of his fall. And tasting the blood in his mouth, he thought how maybe a ruined tooth was not all that important anyway.

A Tale of Two Cities

1.

London

HIS MOTHER ANSWERED the phone. She said he'd gone away for the weekend. She said she thought he'd told me, and I said maybe he had, that it must have slipped my mind. I didn't want her to hang up, so I said, 'How are you anyway, Mrs. Atkins?'

'Oh, not too bad, thank you.'

I came straight out with it and asked her if Keith had told her anything about Estonia. He hadn't. What, nothing? Absolutely nothing? Nothing about him coming away with me, nothing about any plans the two of us had for moving to another country? It was like the planning had all been in my head. She sounded completely innocent. I doubt she'd even heard of Estonia.

'It's just that I've got a job there – in Estonia. I'll be going away at the end of the summer.'

'That'll be a bit of an adventure.'

That's all she said. Well-trained. Or which way round was it? Was the son the product of the mother or the mother the handiwork of the son? I saw them as both equally dishonest.

'Anyway, nice talking to you,' I said. 'Take care.'

I don't know why I said that. Why would I want her to take care? What did I care about her? It's something I say when I don't know what to say, or when I *do* know what to say, but know I shouldn't. When I put back the receiver, I saw my hand trembling and I thought, *That's not me. That's not my hand trembling.*

I
Palermo

The apartment they used was in the *Centro Storico*. It belonged to Enzo's friend Salvatore Amato. Like Enzo, he was in the business, though a good deal more successful. Amato had property on Lampedusa and a villa just outside Nice. He was happy to lend his friends the use of his flat in town, his *garçoniere*. His own home was a high-walled villa by the sea in Mondello, bequeathed to him by a Milanese film director in exchange for a favour.

A woman came once a week, usually on a Thursday, to clean the apartment and do the laundry. The *palazzo*, for that is what it was – a palace belonging to an old aristocratic family, converted for filthy lucre into voluminous apartments with frescoed ceilings – had other tenants. They turned a blind eye to the comings and goings on the first floor. Mostly law-abiding city professionals, they wouldn't have wanted to tangle with the likes of Amato or his friends. Had they sneaked a look that evening, they would have seen a tall woman, wearing knee-high boots and a three-quarter length winter jacket in mock leopard skin, her pale face partially obscured by the jacket's hood, and – just visible – a few locks of bottle blonde hair.

Laura couldn't have been more conspicuous if she had tried.

2.
Kensington & Chelsea

I told Amrita how Keith had gone AWOL, and how he hadn't even mentioned to his mother that he was coming away with me to Tallinn. Amrita said Keith was a bastard and had no intention of going anywhere. He was just using me.

'I'll bet he's back with that ex-girlfriend of his,' she said. 'The one from Clapton, or wherever.'

'Weston-Super-Mare.'

'Weston-Super-Mare. What's her name … Sandra, Susan?'

'Sharon.'

'Sharon. Right. She's not so ex, is she?'

I told her that we had no evidence to think that it was about her, about Sharon. We were only guessing he'd gone back to her.

'It's her. You *know* it's her,' she said. 'And most likely a few others too.'

What did she mean 'others?' I was thinking that surely this couldn't get any worse. But it could.

'Mike saw Keith last week in Sloane Square and he was with someone, with "some bird or other."'

'What bird or other?'

'I don't know. Some woman on the same course. Some woman from his History class.'

How come everyone except me seemed to know he was playing the field?

'Why are you so surprised? I'll bet he was doing that all the time he was married. That's probably why he's divorced.'

There are moments when I have flashes of a person as they really are, not the person I thought they were when I first met them. What was Keith after all?

'Come on, Laura, is that really the man you want to be with? A balding fifty-year-old clerk with an unfinished crime novel?'

And then there was the mother. Amrita didn't mention her.

'And don't forget that obnoxious mother of his,' said Amrita. 'Wouldn't you just love to spend time with her?'

Did I want to know that Keith was seeing other women? He didn't look as though he had it in him, but then I'm a bad judge of men. And they're a bad judge of me. So, why did he come after me?

I saw myself reflected in the dressing table mirror, hunched over the phone listening, stabbing the tip of my pen into my address book, punching inky holes into its leather cover.

'Laura?' she said. 'Are you listening to me?'

'It was a relationship,' I said.

'No, it wasn't,' said Amrita. 'You need to call him up and put an end to it. You deserve better. You don't have to stand for this.'

No, I don't have to stand for it. I thought, What do you think? That you're getting away with it? Go to Hell, Keith. Go to Hell.

II

Ballarò

Laura had flown back in after an absence of three months. Her belongings were in storage at Amato's warehouse while she searched for accommodation and a new job. Her prospects were good. Her Italian, which she had studied in Florence, was flawless – better than Enzo's. He struggled when formality required him to use Italian, and he was only at ease when he could revert to his native Sicilian.

On this visit, with barely forty-eight hours gone, they were at each other's throats. Enzo had that dark look about him. He had been silent as they drove to the apartment from her hotel. She knew there'd be trouble. She'd complained about the run-down old pensione he'd booked her into and she'd told him to find her somewhere else. But she knew his ugly mood was not just about that.

'I saw you,' he said.

'Saw what? What did you see?'

'*You* tell me,' he said.

'How can I tell you if I don't know what you're talking about?'

'Don't give me that kind of attitude,' he said.

'What kind of attitude?'

'You know very well. Why don't you just tell me the truth?' He had raised his voice.

'They'll hear next door,' she said.

'Don't change the subject.'

She gave him a look of disgust and turned away. He grabbed her by the arm. He hurt her.

'Don't turn your back on me!' he said.

She pulled away.

'Come here,' he shouted.

She was in the passage, heading for the door. This time she was going. That was it. She wasn't going to stand for these fits of jealousy any more. Why should she?

3

Holland Park

When he finds out from his mother that I've been checking on him, he'll call. Someone called. Was that him? Maybe not. He might have tried me from his home phone. He wouldn't have used his mobile. Would he? Whoever it was, they didn't ring back.

Alison called. Mind reading. She had never liked Keith.

'I knew it,' she said.

'Well, then, you should have told me.'

'I did. I told you that being involved with him was dangerous for you.'

'I don't understand. What do you mean?'

'Emotionally. Dangerous emotionally,' she said.

'What? Are you thinking he might unhinge me or something?'

'No. Just that I don't like to see you upset.'

'I'm not upset,' I said. 'I don't even like him.'

'You don't?'

'No.'

I could hear her moving pots and pans about in the kitchen.

'No, not really.'

'Not really? What about him being the man who couldn't wait to spend time with you, the man who wanted to be with you always?'

'Did I say that? I don't know. I think I put him off.'

After she rang off, I fixed myself an abundant vodka and tonic and set to brooding. There would be no vodka deficit in Estonia. Alone and in a foreign land I could wallow in my sorrows as much as I wanted. I would enjoy that.

Keith was a *bad* liar because his excuses were so elaborate. He was a *good* liar because he said everything with total conviction, as though he truly believed his own stories.

There was still a remote chance that he might come directly to the flat. Would he have her perfume on him? Once before, he had gone to his daughter's for the weekend. We were supposed to be going to Alison's. At the last minute, he'd come back weary and creased. I should have been more attentive. I should have noticed the clues. It does, after all, take a certain stamina to lead a double life.

III

Casa Professa

Enzo was behind her as soon as she had her hand on the latch. He slammed the door shut before she could open it wide enough.

'Leave me alone,' she shouted and, pushing past him, she turned back in her tracks towards the lounge, her heart pounding. She felt fear and hate combined.

He stepped after her, reaching for her shoulder.

'Don't touch me,' she said and, even as she spoke, she saw the bronze glint of the candle holder. Her hand brushed the cold marble surface of the ancient dresser, her fingers slipped around the candelabra's brass base. The thought flashed through her mind that in a moment it could all be over. She lifted it high into the air. *How heavy it was.* And then she reeled around, sweeping it down towards his head with all the power and strength in her body. She had a sense, a momentary awareness, of doing wrong. She did it anyway. He deserved it.

4

Norland Square

Alison kept saying how sorry she was about Keith. Sorry that he'd been caught out? Sorry that I'd realised he was a waste of space? No, she was glad really. Like me.

I laughed. 'It's appalling, isn't it?' I said to her. It was like I'd paid out good money and got a dud, and I was saying, *It's okay. Now I know, and it didn't cost me much anyway.* It would have been far worse if I'd got pregnant, or if I'd married him. Imagine. No, don't imagine.

From wanting total commitment, Keith had backed off. One moment he was talking as though he wanted to spend the rest of his life with me, then he'd stopped. He'd got cold feet. And I was still thinking that having had him was like having had a husband, someone whose heart was mine, who was on my side, on my team.

Such a romantic.

I'd wanted his success as much as my own. But I had broken my own golden rule. I had trusted him. Or was I being a trifle melodramatic here? *Boo hoo! She'd trusted him.*

Now that I was seeing it in perspective, it didn't seem right that I'd be working my butt off while he was sitting in our little flat in Tallinn doing his writing – his stupid crime novel, his Elmore Leonard rip-off. If I had wanted the perfect formula for becoming stressed and resentful, this was it. Now I would be going it alone.

It's really not a good idea to send a woman away on her own to a foreign country. She'd be a liability, like a daughter who should be married off before she creates mischief. How many tries are you allowed in your life? Can we create mischief more than once? Do we get better at it?

IV

Salita Raffadali

She washed her hands in the bathroom, staring at her face in the mirror. What had this person done? Why did she look so calm? What next? Trembling, she looked around for anything of hers that was in the apartment. Nothing. She checked the kitchen. There was a San Pellegrino bottle on the table. He had opened it. She left it as it was. On the coffee table in the lounge was his glass of whisky, hardly touched, and her glass of Aperol. She picked up her drink – leaving his – carried it to the kitchen, emptied out the glass, washed it, dried it carefully, put it in the cupboard, straightened out the damp teacloth, walked out of the kitchen. Then, doubled back with some toilet tissue from the bathroom. She wiped the kitchen tap. She retraced her steps all around the apartment, erasing prints where she thought she might have left them. She stepped over his body – over the small jelly-like puddle of blood that had pooled around his head – to reach the candle holder. She held her breath as she cleaned it where she had gripped it, and then left it there where it had fallen.

She stood in silence by the door. She heard only the sound of her own breathing. Once she left, there would be no turning back. She stopped in the doorway. She waited to remember what she had forgotten. She saw his keys on the dresser. She scooped them up and left.

5

Slough

He was back from the dead. Pity. I'd just put the phone down from talking to Alison when I saw his number come up on the caller ID display. I couldn't not answer.

His tone was submissive. 'So, are you going out to dinner tonight?' he said. He'd remembered my earlier plans. He wasn't *that* stupid.

'Yes,' I said, 'I'm going over to Alison's.'

'Good,' he said. 'That's a good idea. So, shall I call you tonight?' he said.

'No,' I said.

'No, you won't be in, will you?' he said.

'No.'

'Right then,' he said. 'Shall I call you tomorrow?'

'Yes.'

'All right then. I'll call you tomorrow.'

'Okay.'

'Well, bye then,' he said.

'Bye,' I said.

Our conversations had come to this.

V

Via Mario Puglia

She took the stairs. No one would be coming in or out at this hour and, in any case, there were no tenants she knew of who would choose not to take the lift. She monitored her feelings. To her surprise she felt no remorse, no shock. It was as if she had been able to switch off her emotions. She had had to do what she did. She was defending herself. At the bottom of the stairs, she slipped into the shadow and circled the courtyard to the outer door. From here, had it been day, she would have been clearly visible, but at night the occupants of the apartments closed their shutters. Bars of light shone out from their windows onto the cobbles. Reflected onto the wall to her left were moving figures from the professor's apartment on the second floor. Before releasing the door latch, she waited. The French windows that led out onto his balcony were open. He had only to look over the balustrade to see her. She tensed. She could hear his voice vibrating, shouting through the stillness. An argument with his girlfriend. She heard the shrill voice of the woman. She relaxed, knowing that they were both too wrapped up in their own domestic wrangle to notice the snap of the lock. She stepped out into the narrow street and pulled the courtyard door shut behind her.

6

Kensington Gardens

He wanted to go to the South Bank.

'But that's where we were yesterday,' I said.

'No, we were on the North Bank,' said Keith. He had a much better sense of place than I had. It was raining and, although I agreed that it would be good to go out, I couldn't rustle up much enthusiasm about where to go. When it came to planning how to get from A to B, I gave the impression of being someone who preferred not to make an effort. I was done making an effort. Under pressure, I'd move if I had to.

'I'm thinking Natural History Museum,' I said.

'Why there?' he said.

'Because I want to see some dinosaurs.'

'You'll just see a heap of bones,' he said. 'That's what you'll see.'

It wasn't far, only the other side of the park, but once he said he'd take me, I went off the idea. I didn't really know what I wanted. Something a little more stimulating perhaps. It's funny how we so often long for a peaceful untroubled life and then, when we've got it, we find we want our old troublesome life back again.

He hung his jacket on the back of the kitchen door and went to the bathroom, leaving me to think about where I wanted to go. I checked his pockets, took out his mobile phone and keyed in 'S' for Sharon. I wrote down her number, and switched on the electric kettle. When he came back down from the bathroom, I gave him a nice hot cup of tea.

'If I suggest Covent Garden, you'll say you go there practically every day,' he said.

True. Why would anyone want to go to Covent Garden?

We set out in the rain for Safeways. I had decided I would in any case ensure our supper. He was going to drive round and then pick me up, but the traffic was so heavy that he parked and collected me on foot with the umbrella. We left the shopping in the car and went for a walk in the drizzle. What else was there? We walked through some side alleys – mostly deserted, across Church Street, across Millionaires' Row until we reached the front of Kensington Palace. It gave him a chance to rant on about the canonisation of Diana.

'The Catholics have got it right,' he said.

'I'm Catholic,' I said.

'Lapsed,' he said.

'All right. Lapsed.'

'In your religion,' he said, 'people don't get canonised until hundreds of years after their death.'

'Are you sure about that?'

'Joan of Arc didn't become a saint until the 1920s. I bet you didn't know that, did you?'

I didn't. I didn't much care about knowing either. We went for a long walk in Kensington Gardens. He said he'd decided to go back to the History class for the last two weeks of the term. His tutor – drinking partner – had called him and said he could sit in without paying. One more thing he was getting for free. The thought occurred to me that if he went back to the class, I'd be on my own in the evenings. I felt a pang of envy and resentment. What *was* this? Had I become relationship-dependent? I had never had a problem before about occupying my time. But this was Keith consolidating his connections. He was re-creating his own world of which I was not a part. Old feelings were shaking themselves awake and coming back to haunt me.

We sat on a bench, we watched people walking their dogs, and he started talking about his family – about his sister, about his brother-in-law, his daughter, about the son he rarely saw, about his ex-wife and, of course, his mother. Maybe this sharing of personal information was his way of placating me. I listened without commenting. His sister's family always went down to Dorset for their holidays, he told me. He was going to take his mother down there on Saturday.

I looked at him. 'Saturday?' I said. 'This Saturday?'

He said it would take about an hour and a half.

'I'll come back Sunday,' he said. 'I mean, Saturday. I'll come back the same day.'

I looked at him. He looked at me.

'You don't believe me, do you?'

For a moment I thought he might actually be telling the truth, but it didn't really matter anyway.

As calmly as I could I said, 'So, you'll come to my place when you get back?'

He started calculating the time. 'Let's see. That's an hour and a half, then I'll have to stay for a bit. Then the time to get back ...' He paused. 'Yes,' he said.

Was he really the devoted son or were these more lies?

'How long do you think your mother's going to be around?' I asked him. 'Is she going to live a long time?'

For a moment, he looked startled. One eyelid twitched.

What? Did I say something wrong?

'Well, my auntie lived until she was ninety-six,' he said, 'and my uncle died in his seventies, but he had cancer ...'

'Basically you think she's going to go on for a very long time,' I said. 'You're going to have to look after her, aren't you?'

'Unless I move out,' he said. 'I think that if I moved out, my sister would move in.' He thought for a moment and then he said, 'I think one of the reasons I got married ...'

'Was to get away from your mother,' I said.

'Yes,' he said.

Yet she'd got him back again after the break-up of the marriage.

'I've told you all about me,' he said. 'I still don't know much about you though, do I? Not really.' He had that puppy dog look. His big brown eyes looked soulfully into mine. I couldn't have despised him more.

'I'm just a simple book editor with a passing interest in history,' I said. 'What you see is what you get.'

'I always look forward to getting what I see,' he said.

Did he snigger when he said that, or what?

VI

Piazza Bologni

She walked purposefully down the alleyway to the nearby piazza where Enzo had parked his car. The buildings surrounding the square were for the most part government offices and closed at this hour. A small bar situated on the far side, at the junction with the main road, was still open and a group of four or five men were playing cards, far too preoccupied to notice the slight figure of a woman sliding into the driving seat of an Alfa Romeo. She reversed out from between two vehicles and did not switch on her lights until she had entered the narrow street that led to the Via Maqueda.

She turned left into another small street and stopped the car. She opened her suitcase inside the boot and she plundered the contents as swiftly as she was able, throwing only the indispensable into Enzo's battered hold-all. She bundled up the first few items, a skirt, some jeans, a favourite shirt, and dispersed them inside a nearby bin. She slipped off her coat, ripped out the lining, tore away the hood and deposited the pieces in a skip at the end of the road. She continued in this fashion until she reached the Via Roma. She replaced her coat with a denim jacket, selected from what remained in the case. She changed into a pair of flat walking shoes. She pushed her hair back behind her ears.

She stopped the car one last time, removed the labels from the suitcase, twisted it back on its hinges and left it beneath a heap of other rubbish, old plastic chairs and a broken table stacked high against an unplastered brick wall. A brown furry creature ran out across her path as she disturbed the pile. She was unperturbed.

7

Weston-Super-Mare

'Hello, Keith, it's Laura again, calling at 6:15. Just wanting to know how you are.'

It was more or less as I had thought. On Saturday night when I got back from Alison's, I called him. He wasn't in. I called the mobile and it was switched off. I called his home. There was no reply.

I called him at half-hourly intervals on his home phone, and at hourly intervals on the mobile. There was no reply at home and the mobile was still switched off. I left messages.

He couldn't blame anything on the car again. He had raved on Friday about how well it was going since he and Tony had repaired it. He babbled on at me about how he was using Routemaster directions to get to Poole. I suppose the Routemaster must have gone wrong and he had ended up in Weston-Super-Mare by mistake.

The next stage of this adventure was for me to phone Sharon. I was undecided. I imagined the scenario. When she answered, I'd say, 'Sorry to disturb you. This is Keith's sister Carol. Could I have a word with Keith, please?'

There were two possibilities. In possibility one, Sharon would say, 'I'm afraid he's not here, Carol. I haven't seen him.' In which case I'd say, 'Sorry, love, I couldn't think where he'd be. The mobile's switched off, you see. I called his girlfriend's, but he's not there either, so I thought I'd try you. He'll probably turn up sooner or later.' End of conversation. I'd hang up.

The second possibility. I'd ring up at 9:00pm. Sharon would answer. I'd say, 'Sorry to disturb you. This is Keith's sister Carol. Could I have a word with Keith please?'

She'd say, 'Oh, yes, Carol, just a minute, I'll get him.' I'd hear the rustle of sheets. She'd be passing the phone across the bed and saying, 'It's Carol for you.'

I'd hear his voice. He'd be saying, 'What?' There'd be a bit of fumbling about. He'd come on the line, and he'd say, 'Hello?'

Then I'd say, 'Hello, Keith, I've been trying to get hold of you, but the mobile's switched off.' I'd say, 'Did you get lost? I thought it was Poole you were going to.'

There's nothing worse than a lying lover.

VII

Via Lincoln

From Via Roma she turned left into Via Lincoln. She identified his father's apartment immediately. It was set above a fabric store, and she recognised the ornate wrought iron balcony that overlooked the street. Since his father's death, he had regarded this shabby little apartment almost as a safe house, escaping there from time to time to avoid pressing responsibilities, his wife, his in-laws, unwelcome business associates.

She cruised past once, twice. When she was sure no one was in the vicinity, she switched off the lights and parked in the gutter at the front of the building. Before getting out of the car, she sprayed a little Calèche in the air, just a touch. He had given her the same perfume he gave to his wife.

She collected up the holdall, did a last check, locked the car door and, keeping to the shadows, walked briskly in the direction of the port, dropping his keys into a drain a hundred yards or so down the road.

8

Abbotsbury Road

I felt sure that if I called Sharon's, he would be there. I just needed the strength to do it. I needed a sign to do it. I thought, *Show me a sign. Show me a sign.* I went into my bedroom and fiddled with my hair. I looked around thinking I might see something out of the window, a squirrel in a tree, or something – I don't know what. There were people about doing various things, street-cleaning, delivering food, someone carrying luggage into a hotel across the road. Then I saw a woman jogger coming laboriously along the street. I thought she might as well give up there and then for all the good it was doing her. She turned and headed up Abbotsbury Road. On the back of her baggy tee-shirt, I saw a huge letter 'S.'

The phone rang for a long time. I thought, *Now she'll answer,* and then the answering machine came on and I heard her voice: there was no one there to answer my call, blah, blah, it told me. She had an ordinary voice. It wasn't particularly youthful. It sounded like the voice of a fifty-year-old woman. It was a strong voice, but a very bland voice. I waited until the message was almost over and then I hung up. In a way it was a relief. There was nothing more I could do. I called Amrita.

'What news?' she said.

'I told him I was seeing someone else.'

A pause.

'My God!' she said. 'Good for you. How'd he take it?'

'I think he got the message.'

'What about Tallinn? Are you still going?'

'Yes. Alone.'

And then I called Alison and, as I told her of the break-up, my voice failed me and tears welled up in my eyes.

Alison listened without commenting. Then she said, 'The man is seriously ill. He's emotionally sick. You've had a very lucky escape, Laura. He'd have destroyed your life if he'd gone to Estonia with you. I know it's hard right now,' she said, 'but just let it go. In two or three weeks you'll know what you did was right. Keith obviously thought he was on to a good thing,' she said. 'Here is a lovely woman, with a home and an income. He was thinking what was in it for him. He is vain. He is selfish.'

I was the mug though. I was the one who had lost face in front of my friends.

'What's happening about him going with you to Tallinn?' she said. 'They'll be expecting the two of you.'

'I've written to them,' I said. 'I've told them I'll be taking up the post *sans* partner.'

'Single status, then.'

'Yes, single. Very single.'

VIII

Via Francesco Crispi

When she bought her ticket for Genoa, the man behind the counter looked at her curiously. He spoke to her in Italian, nodding his head in the direction of her camera bag.

'Enjoy your holiday?' he said.

'Certainly did,' she said.

'You're Florentine, if I'm not mistaken.'

'How did you know that?' she said, feigning amazement.

'Ha!' he said, tapping the side of his nose. 'I'd know that accent anywhere. My sister-in-law's from up there. It's better down here though, don't you think? You can't beat the south for hospitality.'

She laughed in agreement, gathered up her ticket and her change.

'Have a good trip, signora,' he called after her.

'Signora?' Was she so changed? So much older? Then she remembered the ring. She slipped it off her finger. What else had he noticed? She went to the bathroom. In her make-up bag, she found a few clips and an elastic band. She pinned up her hair as best she could. She wrapped a scarf around her head, then thought again and undid the scarf. No point in exaggerating. It was best to keep things simple. She made her way to the waiting room.

A young couple with their two children sat in a far corner of the room. For the first time since she had left the flat, there was nothing more to do. She stared at the wall and the windows in the wall, and the blackness of the night behind the windows. It occurred to her that she had nothing to read. How could she read? Hadn't she just killed a man? And, if she had just killed a man, why did she feel no regret? None whatsoever.

9

Queensway

I ate at Alison's at lunchtime and drank quite a lot of red wine. It was partly because her brother was there and I had taken a shine to him. I was drinking wine to make me feel more relaxed, but not just because of him.

Come the evening, the wine had rotted my guts and I regretted it. I needed to be on form. Keith called me on his mobile from Shepherd's Bush.

'Almost there,' he said.

I said why didn't we just go out for a drink. I knew he'd agree to anything. He waited outside for me in the car. I got in and off we went. He was in one of those irritating, 'I'm game for anything' moods.

'Where are we going?' he said.

'Queensway,' I said. 'I'll tell you where.'

'Queensway? Not Soho then?' He thought he was being funny.

We parked the car in a street full of hotels to the back of the Bayswater Road. It was a muggy, humid evening. People were sitting out on doorsteps and the pub-goers had spilled onto the pavements.

'Why don't you leave your jacket in the boot,' I said. 'I can put the car keys in my bag.'

'Oh, all right then,' he said. He opened the boot, then handed me the keys. He took his mobile phone and his wallet out of his pocket. 'I suppose you want my wallet too, do you?' he said, like a naughty husband who was having his finances monitored.

I thought, *You plonker*!

He wrestled out of his jacket, folded it elaborately and stowed it away.

'All yours,' he said, shutting the boot with a flourish.

I looked around to check if anyone had been watching. In Palermo, I would have got back in the car and parked it somewhere else. Someone was always hovering to see if you were going to leave something thievable behind.

I walked him in the direction of the club. I glanced at my watch. We were still in good time.

'Looking forward to Tallinn,' he said.

'Are you?' I said.

'All those coffee shops. Men in overcoats and trilbies. I'm going to enjoy it. Do you suppose they sell Marmite over there?'

'No, I don't think so,' I said.

'You seem tense,' he said to me.

'No, I'm fine,' I said. 'What about you?' and I looped my arm through his. I guided him into the series of alleys. We passed a nest of tables where people were sitting outside eating, the smell of garlic and roast calamari wafting out into the dense summer air.

He said, 'Where are you taking me?' and then, looking about him, as if suddenly inspired, he slid into a narrative, along the lines of: '*She turned into a dark cobbled street away from the bustle of the club area. In the dim light, he could see only that the road was closed off by buildings at the end. To his left was a doorway, the service entrance of another building whose front was on the main thoroughfare. Two men stood in the doorway, waiting. This would have been a good place to bump him off.*'

'I wouldn't do that, would I, in front of a bunch of people eating out at a Greek restaurant?'

He said, 'That's how the Mafia do it.'

'Really?' I said. 'You could be right then.'

⇥⟶ ⟵⇤

Swimmers

Villa 109, Between the Two Bridges, Abu Dhabi, November 2010

1

I FIRST MET Neville Dickens at a luncheon party in Wimbledon. I believe the year was 1992. I have always thought 'party' to be a rather inexact description. Margaret's house in Copse Hill was hardly a hotbed of drunken ribaldry. Lunch was a mild affair with just Margaret, Henry and the taciturn playwright with the literary name. Margaret never did anything without a reason. In the kitchen over a glass of sherry and steaming vegetables she confessed that since I wrote, or – rather – dabbled in screenplays, she had decided that I simply *must* meet this young radio drama writer of hers. For young, she intended someone younger than herself. Neville was all of forty-three if he was a day. Naturally he was recently separated from his long-term partner – fortunately female, which was rare in these circles. Margaret dealt in re-bounding men and sought to repair my single status.

'But it suits me very nicely, thank-you, Margaret,' I told her.

'Nonsense,' she said, 'every woman needs a soulmate and you, Helena my dear, aren't even trying.'

I could have told her there and then that it does not do to match-make two rival talents. It had all the hallmarks of a very bad mistake.

As I recall, I had a not-insubstantial ability to write, and my output in those days was prolific. Now, sixteen years on, I have perhaps achieved some minor acclaim as the editor of an in-house publication entitled *The Oil and Gas Journal*, but the early promise of Baftas and Oscar nominations now seems but a foolish aspiration. As the wind swept through the date palms, as the muezzin called the faithful to prayer, and as I prepared my usual solitary supper of hummus, olives and sambosas, an announcement on the BBC World Service – my only remaining link with the world as I had known it – caught my attention. A new radio production was soon to be broadcast, featuring Kristen Scott Thomas, Peter O'Toole and Jonathan Rhys Myers, and written by the playwright Neville Dickens, author of the 1995 adaptation of Proust's *A la recherche du temps perdu*. With some small measure of melancholy, I found myself revisiting that lunchtime meeting in South-East London.

When Margaret and I rejoined the men in the living room, Henry was telling Neville all about Egypt. He had got to the bit about Cairo. Henry and his colleagues had taken to playing with a Ouija board in the evenings. Lawrence Durrell joined them.

'He was always good company,' said Henry, 'but he could be decidedly awkward at times.'

"You're pushing the glass," he told Henry.

"No, I'm not," said Henry, "it's moving of its own accord."

They started to get messages. Lawrence wrote them down while Henry and the others kept their fingers on the glass. Eventually it did actually spell out a name – that of a Polish airman, killed in action.

'Jolly curious,' Henry told Neville.

'I wonder what he wanted,' said Neville.

'Who?' said Henry.

'The Polish airman.'

'I couldn't say,' said Henry.

'Tell them what happened next,' said Margaret.

I could not help thinking this interference in the afterlife may well have addled Henry's brain, and had I been Margaret I would not have encouraged him in these other-worldly recollections. Neville, on the other hand, showed every sign of one keen to hear the next instalment.

Henry related that one day, when he was the one doing the writing, a very important message came through.

It said, "You must take Arnold to a green place, or something terrible will happen."

'That's an awfully long message to spell out on a Ouija board,' I said, but I was silenced by Margaret who gave me a sharp nudge in the ribs with her elbow.

'Who was Arnold?' asked Neville.

'Oh, he was someone we knew,' said Henry. 'He hadn't been at all well... trouble with his wife, you know. His nerves were bad.'

'And did you take him to a green place?' I asked.

'No, we didn't,' said Henry, raising his eyebrows as he contemplated his sherry. We all waited, but Henry was not forthcoming.

'So, what happened next?' asked Neville.

'Something terrible,' said Henry. 'He threw himself out of a fifth floor hotel room in Cairo. I suppose if we had taken him to a green place – away from his wife – that would never have happened. Poor old Arnold,' he said. 'Another glass of sherry, Neville?'

Lunch beckoned and once we were seated, Margaret worked feverishly to find our common denominator.

'Neville is working on an adaptation of Proust,' she announced, looking pointedly at me. 'For the BBC,' she added.

'Oh gosh!' I said, taking the cue, 'it must be monstrous piece of work. Doesn't it frustrate you to be constantly assailed by the creation of others?'

Margaret glowered at me.

'Not at all,' said Neville. 'It's what I do. I adapt.'

'Perhaps you should try that yourself, Helena,' said Margaret.

'I've written an *original* radio drama,' I said. I put the emphasis on 'original.'

'I thought you wrote screenplays,' said Henry. 'Didn't you tell me that Elizabeth wrote screenplays, Margaret?'

'Helena,' said Margaret, somewhat fraught.

'Eh?' said Henry, who was on his feet now, refilling the wine glasses.

'It's Helena, Henry. Not Elizabeth,' said Margaret.

Neville coloured slightly. Our eyes met across the serving dishes.

Margaret thought fit to change the subject. 'The Polish airman came back of course, didn't he, Henry?' she said.

Henry paused. 'Did he?' he said. 'Are you sure?'

'Don't you remember?' said Margaret. 'That was how we met. He said, "You shall go to the land of the Kikuyu." That's what he said, and that's what you did and that's how you met me.'

'Ah, yes,' said Henry. 'I suppose he spoke English, did he?'

'Helena's going to Kenya next week. Isn't that right, Helena?' said Margaret.

'Business or pleasure?' asked Neville.

'Both,' I said.

'I lived there in the fifties,' said Margaret, 'at the time of the Mau Mau. We didn't have air conditioning then, of course. We just had our mosquito nets and put wet towels around our necks at night to keep cool. The people upstairs had a ceiling fan and we thought that a great luxury, quite grand.'

'I have things to do in Nairobi,' I said, 'and the Aberdares.'

'At that time, of course, Nairobi was very elegant,' said Margaret. 'The women dressed as if they were shopping in Bond Street or lunching in Belgravia. We lived on the coast. I shopped in the market and bought the local meat like everyone else. I took great care over where I went and what I ate. No ice in my G & T, which was a bore, but then I never had any problems with mosquitoes or tummies or anything else for that matter. I brought up two children there. Nothing wrong with them.'

'Goodness,' I said, 'I hadn't thought of the food. Do you think I ought to take something?'

'Carbon tablets should be fine. Imodium is, I think, a little severe. Have some more of the roast, Neville,' she said. 'You're not eating.'

I passed the meat to Neville, who declined.

'Now the Americans,' continued Margaret, 'they were the ones who went down with things. They came kitted up with everything under the sun – malaria tablets, all the latest inoculations, instructions about what not to eat – and they went down like flies.'

'I suppose I had better take a bug spray with me too,' I said and I smiled coquettishly in Neville's direction.

2

'What's it about?' said Neville. 'Can you pitch it to me?'

'An elderly writer falls in love with a young woman – his publisher. She is flattered and intrigued by his attention, but she is dissuaded from involvement by her friends who tell her he is far too old for her. She takes their advice and distances herself from him.'

I stopped here and waited for his comments.

He thought for a moment.

'Is it autobiographical?' he said.

'Heavens no!' I exclaimed. I felt the Parry-Shaw temper rising. 'Why do you suppose that it cannot merely be born of the imagination?'

He raised an eyebrow. 'How does it end?' he said.

'Suicide. The writer drowns himself.'

He blinked, and then stared at me intently.

'Can I read you just the first few lines?' I said. 'I don't want to bore you.'

'You could never bore me,' he said. 'Go ahead.'

I began.

Neville listened, his eyes downcast, as he smoked his cigarette, taking an occasional sip of whisky.

I thought, is my story dull?

I continued.

He stubbed out his cigarette, not looking at me. There was a silence during which I remember thinking it's awful and he doesn't know how to tell me.

He looked up. 'It's very good,' he said. 'Excellent, in fact. Is it all like that?'

'I couldn't say. That's for the listener to judge.'

'It's economical. Very Pinter.'

'It's not Pinter. It's Parry-Shaw.'

'What's this play of yours called?' he asked.

'*Swimmers*,' I said.

'Curious title. Why's that?'

'In a relationship,' I said, 'when things get rough, we have to swim, keep from drowning. We have to save ourselves. My character Michael could have saved himself, and the woman, Susan, could have saved him.'

He stared at me for a moment.

'I'll read it,' he said.

'You're not just saying that because I've got you into a tight corner?'

He held out his hand to take the typescript. 'I wish you *had* got me in a tight corner,' he said, and as I handed over the pages, his hand touched mine.

'I'd like to invite you home for a nightcap,' he said.

It was, in short, a lapsus, though a spontaneous and pleasurable one. I left for Nairobi two days later and it was only when I returned after an interval of three weeks that I realised that, while he had my number, I did not have his. Margaret and Henry were with friends in Tuscany for the holidays. I renounced the idea of tracking him down. I did the next best thing. I forgot him.

3

The night of the radio play I dreamed that I was trapped in the revolving door at Broadcasting House. A group of Kikuyu tribesmen danced rhythmically on the other side of the glass while I looked around desperately for a lavatory. Neville was in there somewhere, peeling pages like the leaves of a banana tree off the top of my manuscript. I knew it was my manuscript because my name was printed in red ink in the centre of each sheet. *Helena Parry-Shaw, deceased,* it said. And as I pondered this error I heard the Polish airman grumbling about the expense of flying a star-studded cast all the way to Nairobi to record a radio play about a failed and ageing female screenwriter who had fallen for a man half her age. When I awoke, I began to cry. How I loathe dishonesty!

At my desk, in the early hours of the morning, I re-read the letter I had drafted the night before to the World Service Radio Drama Section. I had no choice now but to set out to prove the truth.

"In conclusion," I wrote, "I, Helena Parry-Shaw, am the true author and creator of the work that you broadcast last night in your *World Drama* series. The work that I crafted sixteen years ago, and that my life was given to, has been

maliciously counterfeited, deconstructed, transformed. This fraudulent repro-
duction of my play by Neville Dickens, who has changed the title of the work
from *Swimmers* to *Divers*, is nothing more than a monstrosity, a grotesque and
abominable fake."

And outside, as my thoughts returned to Wimbledon, I heard only the distant crowing of a cockerel and the rustle of the palms.

Great Expectations

Skincare secrets

THIS WAS WHEN Julie first took account of Miranda. Maybe it was sometime around 1967. It couldn't have been earlier because Julie's grandmother was already dead at this point and the memory of her own mother crying at the kitchen table for her loss was just that – a memory.

This was summer, and it was unnaturally hot. The windows of the classroom were open, but the air hardly stirred and the gauze curtains rustled only a little above this empty West London street. Siestas of sorts were in progress. The girls were drowsy, except – that is – for Julie who was studying Miranda, while Miranda studied Miranda in her make-up mirror, speaking knowledgably about the use and misuse of soap on the skin and how she always applied cold cream before 'putting on my make-up to go out.' Miranda cast a glance at Julie. To gauge her reaction? For such a smallish person, Miranda had the harsh assertive voice of someone who knew with absolute certainty that she was always right. Julie had decided then and there that she did not like Miranda, and that she despised Miranda also for her busy social calendar. She did indeed imagine Miranda readying herself for a soiree, her hair in curlers, her face coated in cream, the translucent pallor of her skin faintly bluish around her eye sockets. Pale lashes, grey eyes, the iciness of her.

Miranda went on continental holidays, returning as white and as cool as the cold cream she smoothed onto her face. Julie saw a Miranda sitting immobile under a parasol, the sand scarcely touching her toes. Her hair would be as it was now, carefully coiffured. This was a Miranda who did not perspire from her tiny hairless armpits, who was unblemished and waxen. Neat, tidy, without emotion. Miranda was not striking, though evidently she believed she was, and self-belief fosters conviction in others. An important lesson for those with great expectations. Sister Myra saw a strikingness in Miranda that Julie could not fathom. From this moment on – the moment of the skincare secrets – Julie would attribute the lows in her life to Miranda, and possibly also to her own refu-genes.

The principles of marriage

Mother Lelia told the class that people should marry their own kind. It made for disharmony and confusion when different sorts mixed. Fay, Jamaican mother and English father, was in that class, as was Amira, Egyptian father and French mother, and then there was Stefania, Italian father and Scottish mother, and Maya, German mother and Japanese father, and Prabha, Indian father and Irish mother. But, as Mother Lelia spoke these words, Julie knew they referred specifically to her, Polish father and English mother. In later years when she was over this, she decided that Mother Lelia must have been very conflicted. Miranda, Irish mother and Irish father must have been laughing.

Misdemeanors

Rebecca Joseph had done something bad. She had done it in the bushes in the park. Which park and what exactly, Julie did not know and no one was telling. It was another of the mysteries of life. She thought the *park* might be somewhere in Hampstead and the *what* might be linked to the seven pages – 41 to 48 – removed from their Biology textbooks. Julie was sorry it was not Miranda who had been caught out and that it was not Sister Myra who had caught her.

Tolerance

Sister Myra favoured a liberal education. Freedom of speech, freedom of expression, freedom of worship, the welcoming of those of other faiths – Jews, Muslims, Hindus, Buddhists, and a few others she could never remember when she spoke of them in morning assembly. For Julie this was good to know, that she could go far in life if she kept an open mind and was not a Protestant. She thought it a pity that Miranda did in fact come from the right side of Hammersmith.

Holy statue

On the day that Julie and her mother had their appointment with Sister Myra to discuss the decisions that would affect the next ten years of Julie's life, Julie's only ally – the diminutive Sister Frances – sneezed whilst walking down one of the convent's darkened corridors and knocked herself out on a holy statue. Sister Myra had insisted that the lights be dimmed to help reduce the sisters' electricity bill. Had Sister Frances been taller, her collision with the statue would have resulted in a blow to the upper chest instead of a clout to the head. While she lay stunned on the parquet floor upstairs, downstairs in the Lower Sixth study room, Sister Myra told Mrs Jabkowska that Julie was not up to taking 'A' levels. Julie half-believed this to be true, but she wasn't ready to give up her rights. Miranda was not up to 'A' Levels either, but that did not seem to matter to Sister Myra.

Music

'I mean, what are the chances of a music teacher being called Miss Haydn?' said Celia – that same Celia who got her Grade 6 theory while Julie just about managed her Grade 1, thus confirming Sister Myra's expectations. Only much later did Julie, reading *Lives of the Saints* in the convent library, come to learn the story of St. Cecilia and only much later still did she come to appreciate classical music. In her opinion, Miranda would have made a superb St. Cecilia and deserved her same end.

'Mozart would have been better,' said Julie.

Gym

Julie and Stefania skipped gym by sitting on the cloakroom benches with the grey coats and mackintoshes weighing down on their heads. A girl they didn't know from the Lower Sixth drew aside the overcoats like a set of curtains and muttered, 'Another pair of lesbians.' But Julie knew they weren't and she felt bad that someone thought they were.

'What did she mean, lesbians?' said Stefania.

'Never mind,' said Julie. She was thinking that you wouldn't catch Miranda sitting there under those damp, malodorous coats.

Names

It took Julie's mother two months to learn how to spell her married name. Julie thought she'd avoid the same problem for herself by never getting married. Her friend Sarah said that if it came to that, she might think of marrying someone with a simple name. Sarah said she herself wasn't worried about the man's name. She just didn't want him to have small feet. She couldn't abide men with small feet.

So when Julie met Simon at Sarah's birthday party, she looked long and hard at his feet, just in case. She noted how Miranda also looked Simon over. His feet and his name were not important when, two months later, she stole him from Julie at Stefania's birthday party. The question for Julie was … did Miranda steal him because she liked him, or did she steal him because he wanted to be stolen? Was Miranda the culprit, or was Simon at fault? If in doubt, both should be blamed? Or Julie herself if Sister Myra had been privy to any of this, which she had not.

Priests

Dora said she fancied Father Donovan, so Julie paid him some attention. She couldn't see it herself and wondered if that was the best Dora could do. Years later she was to think that maybe this was one of her personal failings, aiming too high, reaching for the unattainable, when maybe she should have taken what was readily available, a fresh-faced boy from a family of impoverished intellectuals. Someone like Simon. But while she knew she was out-classed, she also persuaded herself that Simon had not been good enough for her, especially since he had been so easily enticed away by Miranda.

In the meantime, Father Donovan left the order, or the Church, or whatever and, supposedly, Dora, who never got to sit her 'A' levels, ran away with him, but what they might be running away from Julie could not say. School and Sister Myra possibly. The 'running away' was how her mother had described it.

To Julie's knowledge, Miranda never ran away with anyone. She mostly took and discarded them, Simon being a case in point. Julie never ran away with anyone either, and she thought she might regret it one day.

University

At the Students' Union Saturday night disco, Julie danced with two male acquaintances at the same time. One was Greg Hughes, the lab tech, whose girlfriend looked uncannily like Miranda. The other was Julie's History tutor Michael Brigham-Wright, a figure of some authority. Hughes and Brigham-Wright repaired to the delivery bay at the rear of the building and, against the odds, Brigham-Wright slugged Hughes in the jaw and then gave him a black eye. They settled out of court and Brigham-Wright made a generous contribution to a charity of Hughes' choosing. Oblivious to this incident, Julie left the disco that night with Xavier the Jamaican lithographer from Balham, and went to see his etchings. She also viewed many other artworks in the course of her university life.

A brief history of very early boyfriends

When Julie was eight, she had fallen in love with Geoffrey Brown from White City. He was shorter than her, which at eight, was very short. She remembered him to be funny looking – something to do perhaps with his ears – and he had dull brown hair and a side parting. She gave him up after he tried to kiss her by the bins at the back of the playground.

Although she didn't know it then, she had refu-genes. So, too, did Andrew Kaczmarek, whose mother fed him daily on boiled eggs so that he was both blocked and spotty. When Mrs. Kaczmarek met Julie's mother in the street on the way to the doctor's surgery, she said that she looked forward to the day when their children would return home to build their country.

Julie, who felt unprepared for travel and unspecified responsibilities, kept her mouth shut, listened, and when mother and son had gone their separate way, asked, 'What country?'

To which her mother replied, 'Don't mind her. No one's going back anywhere.'

Perhaps Andrew could have been a boyfriend, but not if he was intending to go back, or was being sent, to build an unknown country. Julie sure as Hell wasn't going.

At junior school, there was Jolyon, who she stabbed in the cheek with an HB pencil during the playground wars. He wasn't so much a boyfriend as a soulmate. The stabbing was an accident, of course. Difficult to say if this was anything to do with the unpredictability of people with refu-genes.

Then there was Simon, but there was also Miranda who took him from her. After that there were the public school boys with big hair, and then the holiday Italians.

For every stolen Simon, two replacements. Multicultural. She doubted that any were Protestant.

Darts

Just when Julie thought she knew nothing, she found she knew something. Even something quite small. Unlike Miranda with her skin-, hair- and nail-care secrets, these insights had come to her late in life.

'You see, because it's baggy,' she said, 'you'll have to put some darts in it.'

'Darts? What do you mean by darts?' said Christine.

If Julie had to, she could pinch together some fabric and sew a dart, but she had never had to. Why would she even bother? She had learnt this at school from Sister Frances, but what use was it to a middle manager who was intending to rise through the ranks? She could do a fair blanket stitch too, and a cross stitch and a back stitch. She had been good at those, at the focus on detail. In this respect, she would surely have surpassed Sister Myra's expectations.

She could play tennis and netball and rounders. She could scramble up a rope and bounce over a wooden horse. She could dance a polka and a reel, and a miscellany of country dances in which she had once dragged her partners through arches of skinny arms, and skipped sideways opposite girls with bouncy bosoms. She could sing a descant and play a recorder. She had learned her Catechism, but couldn't remember it. She thought there was something in there about the Pope being infallible and, that being the case, she wished him well because it couldn't be easy. She had studied French and German – studied not learned – but she could get by. She would have done better if the French teacher, who was also the German teacher, hadn't had such bad BO. She knew some Latin but not Greek, because Greek was for boys, not for girls.

She knew about Caesar's *Gallic Wars*, and about Aeneas. She knew about the Unification of Italy and Cavour. She knew something about Bismarck, but not a lot. Enough. She knew about the patience of Griselda and thought her a fool, especially after reading Germaine Greer. She thought well of Luther because he was constipated from fasting and had a troubled mind. She knew how to light a Bunsen burner, but she had never learned to dissect a frog – for which she was tremendously grateful. She knew about taking the smaller number from the larger number and the sign of the larger number – or was it the other way around?

From Jane Austen, she learned that Darcy was a misery and would remain so, because no woman can change a man who won't be changed. And when Christine had told her that she hoped in time her boyfriend would change, she said that, yes, she agreed. He would change if he had brain surgery. Julie had also read *Persuasion* and understood something of another woman's mind. Not Sister Myra's. But then Sister Myra wasn't a woman as such. Nor was Sister Myra the sort to be admiring the way someone had sewn a dart. Unless it had happened to be Miranda.

'Just get someone to alter it for you,' Julie told Christine. 'Don't waste your time fiddling with it.'

Maps

What Julie also had, she decided, was a sense of direction – physical and spiritual. In the car on the motorway with Sarah, she said, 'Where are we now, Sarah?' which is a question we all need to ask.

But Sarah, significantly panicked said, 'I don't know. I can't find us on the map.' This was in the days before GPS, when Sarah *was* Julie's GPS, sitting with the map on her lap, scanning it, her face contorted, terrorized. 'We have to turn left,' she said. 'We have to turn left. Why aren't you turning left?'

'We can't turn left. We're on the motorway. We have to wait for the exit.' It's always best to wait for the exit. And they motored on, as Sarah wailed, 'But, we're off the map. We're off the edge of the map.'

And that was another thing she knew that Sister Myra would not have expected of her, that the map was not the territory and the territory obviously wasn't the map either, and that Julie had decided she needed to be her own GPS.

Sisters

Julie disliked wimpled women, so when, first, Fatima from Royal Holloway and then Leyla from Manchester, applied for posts as junior sales executives, she gave the job to neither of them. Instead she chose Marcus, who fetched and carried for her, and who brought her the contents of Caroline's waste basket every day at close of business after Caroline had departed for her yoga class. After six months in the company, Julie replaced Caroline as head of marketing. Benefits: car, company credit card, foreign travel business class, and miscellaneous perks. Marcus, she saw now, reminded her too much of Simon – previously lost to Miranda – so she had to let him go.

Endings

Not everything has an ending, she realized. Endings are for stories, not for life, except of course, for death. So, when Julie watched *Twin Peaks* on a borrowed boxed set, and when she got to disc nine and expected the ending on disc ten, it never came, because nine was already the ending. She would never know what happened to Shelley, or if Leo was bitten by poisonous spiders, or if the people at the bank were killed by the explosion in the safety deposit box, or if Agent Cooper would remain possessed and never be himself again, or if the sheriff would find love. What, then, had become of Miranda and of Sister Myra? Of Simon's end, she didn't much care. He was not the issue, she understood now. She understood too that she could only guess at endings, or she could invent them for herself, or at least not be disappointed by expecting them. And perhaps they could be pre-determined if the likes of Sister Myra had anything to do with them.

Return

Who is to say if going back is an act of masochism or a statement of achievement, a look-at-me-I -wasn't-good-enough-for-'A' levels kind of return? The Mirandas of this world go back, but what of the Julies?

What was it that happened to Pip in *Great Expectations*? Maggs – or was it Magwitch? – was lurking behind the gravestones, waiting for the innocent to pass by. If you don't go into the graveyard, there's no story. You have to help your story along. So, like Pip, you sidle in, and when the monster grabs you, you are flipped upside down and the world changes and you see it from another perspective, the ground up, the sky down. Not such a bad idea to change the picture now and then. To twirl destiny around.

Driving her shiny black limo — car phone, leather upholstery — Julie pulled into the convent's stony driveway. A bent and somewhat withered Sister Frances, with the faintest of scars on her forehead, ushered her into Sister Myra's empty sitting room. She would never have recognized Julie, she said, but then neither would Julie ever have recognized her.

The room itself was modest and homely. There were papers and letters on a desk in the corner, a travelling alarm clock on the mantelpiece. Those were the things Julie noticed as she waited for Sister Myra to return from the chapel.

The room was heated by a gas fire, but there was a musky, almost damp smell in the air, of things old and decayed, of memories Julie no longer remembered or cared to remember. On a coffee table were some snapshots. Julie sat down in one of the two worn armchairs and began to examine them. The faces were familiar. Maya, with her husband, she supposed. Celia — so much older now. Stefania, Sarah, Fay … even the disgraced Dora, and there were those whose names she could remember and others she could not. These were all mature women, women with grey hair, wrinkles, husbands, handbags, grown-up children, Chihuahuas, in-laws, twin-sets, houses in Surrey, responsibilities, all of them perfectly brought up, schooled, educated, lives normal and expected.

She flipped to another photo. The door opened.

'Julie, how good of you to come.' She was older. She was wrinkled. She was plumper. But Sister Myra was the same. She had that look that continued to tell Julie she had disappointed.

'It's Miranda,' said Sister Myra. 'Do you see?'

Julie looked down at the picture she held in her hand. Yes, there she was. Miranda. Miranda, who never aspired to 'A' Levels — and who looked just as all the others did.

As Julie learned, life is about stories. A story is a metaphor, and the metaphor means something to you deep down in your dark flowing river of a subconscious. So, if the story is a good one, it will take you with it over the oceans of memory and belief. If it is a bad one, for the rest of your life you will wonder where you went wrong.

'Who would have thought,' said Sister Myra, 'that Miranda would have done so well for herself in life?'

Boyfriends

Every boyfriend has a history. When you are young, this does not occur to you. His history may creep up on you and surprise you. It is likely to be an unpleasant surprise if you are not versed in the ways of boyfriends.

I go far back in time to Milan, where I had one and a half boyfriends. The one was Mario. The half was Livio, who might have become my boyfriend had Mario not claimed me first. 'Claimed' suggests that I was a prize of some sort, but it is important to remember that boyfriends prize you only for a short period, when you are relatively new.

So, Mario was the boyfriend and Livio was the kindly, wistful onlooker. Livio was the lesser of the two. He was second in every way to Mario. Mario had money, intelligence, good looks, an expensive car, his own apartment. Livio had none of these and, in his late twenties, he still lived with his mother.

It was not clear to me what brought these two together. Perhaps Livio enjoyed being around someone who had it all, including a foreign girlfriend. Or perhaps Mario needed to measure himself against someone less successful. In reality, Livio was taller, more genuine in nature and more ruggedly attractive than Mario. Yet he took the role of corporal to Mario's captain. When Mario took me out, Livio came too. I was like a pet poodle. My owner kept me in check while a friendly pet minder kept me amused. And it was in our threesome one evening that we found ourselves together in Livio's home.

Livio was remarkably unlike his mother. She viewed me with suspicion from the moment I was introduced. She spoke no English and, at that time, I spoke no Italian. She chattered constantly to her son and to Mario. Judging by the banter they exchanged, she knew Mario well. He was like a second son to her. And here we have it. She knew his history. I did not. So, now, as she talked to them, she eyed me, she looked me up and down. Mario appeared scornful. He laughed, but closing his eyes and clicking his tongue.

I said, 'What did she say?'

Livio coloured slightly.

'She said,' said Mario, '"Is this another of your women?"'

He barked something back at her. She smirked, looked at me, and bustled back into the kitchen.

'I told her to stop being such a bitch,' said Mario. 'She's always having a dig at me.'

'Take no notice,' said Livio. 'That's the way she is.'

You need to look at the people around the boyfriend. That's what I learned. After that, they both looked different to me. I had seen them one way and now I saw them another way. In life, we have only a small element of the story. The rest we guess, we make up, we find out. The not-knowing is sometimes bliss, sometimes paranoia. In the life of a boyfriend, you may represent a tiny part of a percentage. You are a leaf on a tree and eventually the leaf falls. You have to think – I realise now – that you are the tree and he is the leaf that falls. There are other leaves to take his place.

Alone in his apartment the following day, I did what I had never contemplated doing before. I went through the drawers of his dresser. I opened each drawer carefully and sifted through the contents in a manner that would not raise his suspicions. He was not the kind of man who would even imagine that a woman might take the initiative to investigate him. It took no time at all to find his photos: Mario on beaches, in nightclubs, at restaurants, at rustic lunches. And always by his side, his women: blondes, brunettes, tall and Amazonian, tiny and fragile, home-grown and foreign. A few of the photographs were framed and placed face down in the drawer.

Did Livio's mother see an innocence in me that needed to be informed? Innocence is all very well, but it does you no good.

⊶═◉ ◉═⊷

The End of a Brief History of Several Boyfriends

Acknowledgements

Material in this collection has been previously published as follows:

'Postcard' in The National, UAE, online; 'Designer Baby' in Jotters United; 'Rainshine' in Wasafiri; 'Charmed' in Litro Online, as 'A Cure for Snakebites'; 'The Moon Cat' in Writer's Voice; 'The Older Short-Haired Female' in Bare Fiction; 'Swimmers' in Pen Pusher. 'My Friend Eric' was broadcast by Radio Mansfield.

I am grateful to Rana Asfour of BookFabulous and to the many other members of the Abu Dhabi Writers' Workshop who gave me their support and encouragement. Several of the stories in this collection first saw the light in our disturbingly raucous workshop sessions.

Thanks are also due to Robb Grindstaff for his painstaking editing and for uncovering the obsession I seem to have for Biros, Burgundy, and the name Kate. Any errors in the text at this stage should be attributed to my own relentless fiddling and tweaking.

⊷⟶ ⟵⊶

Janet Olearski is a London-born writer of Polish descent. Her short fiction and poems have appeared in a variety of publications, including *Wasafiri, Litro, The Commonline Journal, Jotters United,* and *Bare Fiction.* She has authored several children's books, among them *Twins, Mr Football,* and *The Sunbird Mystery,* and has one unpublished novel, *A Traveller's Guide to Namisa.* Her second novel, *Foreigner,* was shortlisted for the 2014 Telegraph Harvill Secker Crime Writing Prize. She is a graduate of the Manchester Writing School at MMU, and the founder of the Abu Dhabi Writers' Workshop. Read more at http://www.janetolearski.com